SHOT-BLUE

JESSE RUDDOCK

Coach House Books, Toronto

first edition

Published with the generous assistance of the Canada Council for the Arts and the Ontario Arts Council. Coach House Books also acknowledges the support of the Government of Canada through the Canada Book Fund.

LIBRARY AND ARCHIVES CANADA
CATALOGUING IN PUBLICATION

Ruddock, Jesse, 1982-, author
    Shot-blue / Jesse Ruddock.

ISBN 978-1-55245-340-7
    I. Title.

PS8635.U338S56 2017   C813'.6   C2016-904392-4

Shot-Blue is available as an ebook: ISBN 978 1 77056 474 9 (EPUB), ISBN 978 1 77056 475 6 (PDF), ISBN 978 1 77056 476 3 (MOBI)

Purchase of the print version of this book entitles you to a free digital copy. To claim your ebook of this title, please email sales@chbooks.com with proof of purchase or visit chbooks.com/ digital. (Coach House Books reserves the right to terminate the free digital download offer at any time.)

To Nora, Nathan,
and Georgia

BOOK ONE

She hated the narrow dirt mile between their trailer and town. She wanted to erase it the same way she might spit and rub a number off the back of her hand. Rachel didn't own anything, but it was a lot to carry on soft ground. The mud and gravel road was thawing from the top down. It peeled under her steps like skin off rotten fruit. Its dampness rose into her shirt in a mix of sweat and dew that didn't feel good. She would abandon the table and chairs, the bed and mattress. The lamps were useless; where they were going, there was no electricity. But she couldn't abandon everything. They needed their bags of clothes, a handful of cutlery, and the pair of tins heavy with flour and sugar. In red-licorice cursive, the tins read *Merry Christmas*. But they weren't Christmas tins, she used them all year.

Tristan wasn't allowed to help because he made her think. She didn't need to think but to walk the mile. Yet back and forth to town, thoughts of him persisted, distracting her and biting into her shoulder more sharply than any strap. She thought of how he didn't run for the sake of running like other boys. She couldn't even picture what it looked like when he ran. And he didn't try to lift things just to see if he could. He was ten years old and had never tried to lift her.

Four trips made eight miles, and it was that long before she noticed the skin across her stomach was sore to touch. Stopping in the middle of the road, she pulled her shirt up roughly. She was scratched from the boxes she'd been carrying, written on in crappy graffiti. She missed being touched. Her stomach was never seen now, and it was impossible to imagine that it would be. She lowered her shirt, then lifted it roughly again. She'd forgotten her stomach. She would bend, she thought, and break under her own weight like a wave on this road she hated. She didn't imagine a huge wave breaking, no crest and fall in a crush of white, but saw instead a small wave that slid over itself, each time folding in a thin sheet of light. Shyly, she ran two fingers along one of the scratches to her hip. Then she came back and followed another scratch down to her belt and flicked the buckle. Their trailer was close but Rachel didn't want to get back yet. There was a lesson in being alone. There was something she was being taught. But how she hated that idea, that life would teach her something she needed to know by making her get low.

Tristan knelt on a wooden chair on bare knees and looked out the kitchen window. The road was less a road than a path roughly cut between black woods. It was packed with rocks – they had dug the rocks for their firepit out of the road, pocking it up, which made no difference. The road was like a portage: an opening that lets you in but makes no promise to bring you out on the other side. Maybe it narrowed to a dead end or was blocked by a swamp raised by a beaver dam. Maybe it led to a place they weren't welcome. She walked through the cut slowly and stopped, her dark hair falling across her shoulders heavily, and Tristan imagined that she meant to let her hair sweep the ground as it did. He kept his knees on the chair. Most boys would have run out to meet their mothers. But he knew he couldn't understand. She was always telling him, you can't understand everything.

§

They moved into the boarding house in town, a wide two-storey building set on the one road, two hundred feet from the freight docks. It was painted white a long time ago and now the paint shed in chunks like receipts. The place was famous for this: it was a miracle the siding wasn't bare. If you lived there, flaking paint was part of your weather. It fell like snow when the wind had fingernails. On still days, it floated down like leaves and melted on the ground, forming pools of warm blue-silver. This was the kind of place that survives wars on end because no one bothers to burn it. There was a sign over the porch, *Hotel and Bait*, but for ten months of the year, there were no tourists on Prioleau Lake, so the Hotel and Bait transformed into a cheap place for bachelors.

Tristan stayed in their room while Rachel was out working. Not that she was out, because she was only down the hallway or downstairs, earning their stay by cleaning other rooms and helping at the bar. Knowing their window overlooked the empty lot to the right of the building, she never went there. This lot held the appeal of all open fields: an invitation to wander without the threat of getting lost that's felt twenty feet into the woods. There was only open sky. There were only wild grasses that would split around her waist. But Tristan had the calmest, blackest eyes, and she knew how they worked – same as hers – and if she walked down there, under the window, she would be his trespasser. So she never did that, letting him rule in peace, and she promised herself that at the end of June, when they had to move out, they would go down the lake, and the lake opened wider than any window.

He looked out the window, she was right, or slept on top of the bedspread. He slept when he wasn't tired, which kept him up at night, turning him to the window again. All this meant the beginning of his daydream. Always the same dream, but sometimes he wasn't in the water yet. He was clambering down rocks, cold against his feet. Once he could hear the water, he would pull his shirt off. He might carry himself quickly and dive in, but other times he moved with a dread sense, holding on to his shirt and coming up to the edge, standing there too long. In the dream it was night. If in the dream it was day, then day was dark as night. He would tread water: that was it. There was no horizon; the water and sky were the same solid black, but the water pulled him under, the sky lifted his head. He didn't put up a fight; they fought over him. Sometimes it felt like he could tread forever, kicking at the black in peace. Or, he panicked from the start and there was no relief. Sometimes he had to force himself to dive, feeling so heavy in his legs that he could only imagine them sinking him. Diving like that felt like throwing an anchor over the side but at the last second not letting go. When it was very bad, he told himself that he shouldn't have spit into the air and caught it in his own mouth. He probably shouldn't have done other things he couldn't even remember now.

A small stand of silver birch trees was budding in front of the hotel. There were five, but it seemed like more since each split at the base as a hand splits at the wrist. Because she liked these trees, Rachel took her breaks on the front steps. She didn't want to rush the trees, but she was waiting for them. They would break into shade. Not everything that breaks, she thought, breaks into ruin. Every day, sometimes more than once, she would go to one of the low branches and try to pry open a leaf, to release it from its shell with her fingernails, and this is what she was doing when Codas came to find her.

She didn't see him coming but heard him say, 'Don't you think we should wait?'

'For what?' She didn't turn around.

'For them to come to us? Do you always do things like this?'

'I don't know,' she said.

Her dark hair was tied loosely at her neck, in a confusion of depth that pulled him closer to her.

She rolled a bud between her thumb and finger, cracking the seam. But that was it: the leaf was unformed. Frustrated at her own impatience, Rachel turned to leave, stepping so abruptly that Codas didn't have time to move and they collided.

'We agree then,' he said, saying something to distract from the collision.

'To what?'

'To let things happen.'

'I don't know.'

Rachel tried to step right but he shadowed and blocked her.

'The leaves, you've been trying to make them bloom with your hands. I saw you.'

Rachel withdrew her hands to her hips, then pulled them behind her back and held them there.

'I won't hurt you.'

'I won't hurt you,' she told him.

Codas had always believed that Rachel looked different than other women because of the scar that stretched from her eye. It nicked her left temple then ran down her jaw, tent-covering a depression where a full, round cheek should have been. Once, something in there broke, he thought, or maybe it was broken still. But no, it wasn't the scar or the hollow that made her look different; she looked different because she was. He didn't know how to make her listen to him.

There was nothing special about Codas. Maybe they were the same age, but she was still young. He had never been young. Never a boy and no pleasure to her. She couldn't say what colour his eyes might be. Codas was made of one substance, Rachel thought: poured concrete. She had poured concrete for years at her summer job, helping her father. Its acidity ate away at her hands until the skin shed. Codas looked poured, and when they ran into each other, he felt poured too. It didn't make it better that he was wearing a white shirt tucked in. No one on Prioleau wore white shirts. No one tucked in.

'Leaves don't bloom, do they? Isn't blooming for flowers?' she asked.

'I came here to speak with you. I came specifically.'

She ran her eyes down his pants to the crushed grass at their feet, to the bottom of the hotel steps and up the steps to the door, which stood wide open. She could see down the hall leading to the bar. Her break was over.

'I came all the way,' he said.

He had come from Treble Island, where he owned a piece of land that his father had torn off the bone of what was otherwise an Indian island. In a bend at shore was his propane business. On a hill above stood a small chapel. His father had been a Black Robe and was never supposed to have a woman or child. The woman, he never really had. She gave birth and went south, under what circumstances no one was supposed to guess. People said the son was a graft of the man. And it was as if young Codas had shaped himself to the rumour.

'I came here to see you.'

'I can't imagine why.'

'You can't imagine?'

She wasn't looking at him but at the open front door.

'People talk, Rachel. This place isn't a home for a woman living with a baby.'

'He's not a baby.'

'Where is he? Is he very alone? Have you left him with someone?'

'Very alone? What does that mean? You're alone or not.'

'You know what I mean.' He was offering them protection.

'He likes to be alone.'

'Some people are alone, but not by choice and they don't like it.'

She liked it.

'No one should be alone,' he kept on going.

'I have to tell you that you live alone.'

'I wouldn't if you came, and you can come right now.'

He was proposing something he didn't understand and blushed.

It was embarrassing, she thought. He couldn't even blush properly.

'Why don't you come? You can live in the outbuilding.'

'No.'

'How old is he?'

'Twelve,' she said. Tristan was ten. There were ways that Tristan was weak – he didn't run around and didn't try to lift things – but there were ways he was growing stronger than other boys. There were ways, she was sure, that he was growing stronger than most men.

'You should think for him or someone else might step in.'

'No,' Rachel said, laughing at him roughly.

'I'm trying to help you.'

'But I didn't ask anyone for help.'

'You did by living here.'

'I didn't have anywhere else to go,' she said.

'Exactly,' he said. 'Think about that.'

'If you make me explain myself, I'll be too tired to do anything else all day.'

'You're not okay.'

Rachel smiled beautifully.

'Please don't laugh at me,' he said.

But she wasn't laughing, only smiling.

'Do you see the door? It's open,' she told him.

'Yes.'

'I need to close it. I left it open.'

'What do you think about what I've been saying?'

'My break is over. That's how far ahead I'm thinking.'

'You can have a place to stay.'

She would rub his offer into the ground and bury it shallow. She wanted to bury it right here, unmarked under the silver birches. The leaves, when they finally came, would cast the place in shade, and she would sit casually over the promise she had resisted. No one would know why she loved sitting here so much.

'You need to make a choice.'

But there was the possibility of hard rain, rain for days. The rain could be a dog and dig up the grass. Then his promise would surface more terrible than it had been to start.

'I probably will do something,' she said, mostly to herself. 'I don't know yet.'

'First the door? Let's close it together.'

Pretending to go along was something Rachel knew how to do, though she took no pleasure in it.

Codas closed the door himself, quickly reaching across her. 'That was so easy,' he said. 'We closed it.'

§

The bottom of Prioleau Lake buckled and shoaled but the man driving the water taxi wove through the shallows without looking, rolling a cigarette at his waist. He knew where the rocks were. They shot into the open channel past a thousand islands, inlet after inlet, but to Tristan it was all the same – water led to more water, shore to more shore. Tristan sat with his feet in the air, braced on the bench between his mother and another passenger, a man he'd never seen. His mother's long black hair whipped across his face, into his mouth, and he kept brushing it away. The arm of the man beside him was as wide and warm as a dock plank in the sun, the opposite of his mother's, which was so slight Tristan could feel the nub of her elbow through her coat. His mother always took on the temperature of a room. Outside, she took on the temperature of the sky. She was so cold now that he leaned away from her into the plank arm.

As the boat rounded Treble Island, Rachel thought it might not be so bad to live here. Treble had no farming acres. It was only woods, a wild place, and so nothing less than a paradise or hell, depending on how you felt. She had memories of landing on Treble to go to the trading post with her father. She could still see him drinking on that wide porch. They would stay past sundown, then cross the water home in the dark. Maybe her father stayed late for no other reason than that night ride, flying low over the water blind. Sometimes he did nothing but smoke and drink, not saying anything to the next man. Now and then, many people gathered on the porch, playing music and dancing on the long boards, which bent underfoot with the give of a diving board and made Rachel feel the muscles in her legs. She danced with everyone, not only the boys but also the men and women, and she remembered how their bodies through jeans and loose shirts were hard from work, how she drew in close and took any affection allowed her, and how a bad sunburn could make the cool of evening come on stronger.

As the boat slowed, she smelled the trees. The air snapped its fingers like a smelling salt and seemed to wake her, but from what sleep she didn't know. She held her hand in the air and the air washed her hand. She bent her head and it washed the back of her neck.

The other passengers gathered their bags and stepped off the taxi. Rachel and Tristan were supposed to follow them along the boardwalk through the tall grasses to the trading post, then take the wide path right to the old church land. A cabin was waiting for them. It had no windows, but it did have a stove. It had a door they could open to move the air, Codas had said. But Rachel didn't follow the crowd up the boardwalk through the grasses, not even with her eyes. She looked out at the water and tried to imagine how deep it was, and how many islands lay just below the surface.

Tristan held on to the bench with both hands as they jerked into reverse and pulled away from the dock. Treble Island had come and gone. The boat hit the waves harder without the weight of the other passengers, and he felt each wave as a blow to the stomach. From his stomach a bad feeling rose into his chest and spread across the tops of his shoulders like big hands pressing him down. He was soaring and drowning, or he was crying, that was it.

He closed his eyes as Rachel put her arm around him. She held the top of his shoulder, but it was so small it didn't fill her hand. She'd made this shoulder, but it was smaller than her idea of it. Did she not know him? Not even his shoulder. But she had saved him, and herself. The debt they would have found taking charity on Treble Island was not the kind that could be paid off. It was the kind of debt that could only be forgiven.

'Your island?' the man driving the boat yelled over his shoulder.

Her island.

'What's your number?'

There were hundreds of islands. He knew them by number, even the sliver islands in the shadows of the mainland. In his mind, the islands formed constellations, but he also saw them as single points of light.

'Do you know Ransom's place?' she said.

It was awkward for this man to look at her, she thought. Maybe he wasn't used to looking at women.

'Sure I do,' he said. 'It's through the narrows. You're alone out there.'

She wanted him to keep looking so she could figure him out, but he turned back toward the bow. Maybe his eyes were only good for distances. His clothes hung loose, which Rachel understood. She had grown up around men who wore the same set of clothes all year. When it was late summer or fall, the clothes fit well, but after winter into spring, their pants had to be cinched, and out on the water their shirts were sails. She caught herself looking at the lines of his arms and back, sharp and square. They were the kind of lines that tire because we tire, but are unbending.

He watched the bottom for rocks and asked them to jump to shore from the bow, because there was no dock. Rachel pulled Tristan's hands off his face. He'd been crying, but she would think about that later.

Tristan wasn't the kind of boy who jumped off the bow of a boat, but now he jumped far and landed light, with animal grace, his feet sticking to the wet rock, and he turned back with a smile on his face.

The cabin was like most cabins that far down the lake. There were three holes cut out of the front wall: a door and two windows. There was another hole in the roof for the woodstove pipe. It had been ten years since Rachel had opened the cabin door, and she was surprised to find not disaster but preservation. No trippers or hunters had broken in. The small bed was made, the quilt flat and still blue. Nothing had changed, which was unsettling but confirmed what she most wanted: if no one had been there, then no one was coming.

The chairs were pulled out from the table. She pushed them in. A skeleton the length of an index finger lay on the kitchen counter: a row of pine-needle ribs, a tail, and a skull that bore no features, just a pinched bone. A patch, a badge, of thick grey dust blew out from the top of the skeleton, and it took Rachel a second to realize this was the flesh degraded, burned to ash by time. The fur had not survived. Her instinct was to blow the dust off the counter, to see if it would rise. But she didn't want to breathe it in. It was as if someone had put the mouse there for her to find – why would a mouse climb up on the counter and die under the hanging spoons?

She poured a bucket of lake water down the open handle of the water pump and janked it up and down but no pressure bore. The pump leathers had to be rotten, which in a way was a blessing – it would give Tristan a job to do, carrying water up the path from shore.

It was by the way she washed the windowsills, the table, the chair legs, the floor, that Tristan understood she'd been here before. She could only be this rough with things that were hers. She used too much water, maybe because everything felt so dry. But this was not a garden, he kept thinking, as she kept asking him for more.

Together they pulled out the mattress, beat it with a broom and left it to air. They shook the dust out of the floor rug, dug the ashes from the belly of the woodstove, washed the kitchen utensils in the lake, and dragged the cedar canoe out from under the cabin. The canoe was lacquered in pollen and lichen and looked like it wanted to rot. Tristan watched his mother scrape it clean with the back of a knife, slowly revealing that its hull must have been blood-red once.

To him everything felt like too much. To Rachel it wasn't enough, she wanted to do more work to calm down. When the day ended – the sun set without a show and the pines went black – she was too tired to put the bed back together and decided they would sleep outside on the mattress.

'Here we can do what we want,' she told him.

She wanted to tell him everything. He wanted to tell her that he was hungry.

Tristan fell asleep and didn't dream. There was mercy in exhaustion. Rachel watched his chest rise and fall and couldn't believe how slowly he breathed with such small lungs. Moments passed when it seemed he had stopped breathing at all, and so peacefully that she worried that he would yearn one day, or already yearned, for slower breath still, deeper sleep than this. She thought she saw it in him, frustration at the kinds of feeling they were given. Nothing felt quite as it should. His eyelashes were longer and more beautiful than hers, his hair a little darker. Maybe they were the same, or maybe he would have it worse.

The mattress, the blankets, and their clothes were wet with dew in the morning, and so was their skin, but the quiet of night was in them and they woke happily, smiling at each other. His mother was beautiful, Tristan knew. The hurt part of her face made the rest look more perfect, so he looked back and forth. When they were fully awake, she showed him the mist on the far shore, how it looked like smoke, like the mainland was on fire. The smoke didn't cloud but clung to the land like breath reluctant to leave the mouth and the warmth of the body. She kissed his hair and brushed it with her hand, kissing where she brushed, telling him with her affection that this was where they would try to live.

§

He was told not to touch the mirror on the sill. It was a rear-view mirror snapped out of its shell, something she'd done as a teenager after her face was hurt and she wanted to see. She'd seen it shining on a wrecked car at the garbage dump, a cleared field near town that was scattered with trash and the bristly bodies of hungry black bears. In a hurry, with the nearest loose rock, she'd numbly struck the mirror's casing over and over, until a good piece of the glass spat out on the ground. She'd swept it up. Rachel didn't have any money then and couldn't have asked her father to buy her anything, never mind something as useless as a mirror.

Tristan wasn't listening. He tested its edges to see if they were sharp, the same way he saw the fishermen test their cleaning knives, brushing his thumbnail across the edge at a slight angle, producing a thin white shaving.

Rachel never explained the mirror to him, how she'd taken it everywhere with her, how it had never told her anything she didn't already know. She kept it to resist the habit of looking into it. She didn't talk to him about the past, because she couldn't explain things she'd lost her feelings for. She couldn't begin a story when there was no way of drawing any kind of conclusion. It wasn't time for stories anyway. Spring was breaking and here they were.

Spring was not gaudy on Prioleau Lake, with its stands of pine and lowlands of cedar. There were no flowering trees, no stashed bulbs, no crop of sudden colour. Transplants from the south died. Bulbs and seeds that were not native never broke, only softened and rotted in the ground. Spring was marked instead by the quiet unfurling of ferns with leaves that spread like a thousand maps of places Tristan imagined might exist.

The one shock was the pollen. It came suddenly and late in the season, for a day or two days, spit in concert by ten million red pines. It was no dusting; their windowsills and the threshold of their door were splashed yellow. 'We could butter our toast with it,' Rachel teased him. 'Would you like that?' No, he wouldn't. It was the pollen that first drew him down to the rocks, where Rachel would find him sitting all summer long.

At shore was a pollen spill. The surface of the lake was rimed in a finch-yellow film. Where the water churned, it looked like milk tea. He liked it, it was disgusting, and after finding a dead baby bird in the muck, it was rapture: he would save the next one, and he did, lifting and flicking it out of the sludge with a cedar bough. In a trance, he watched the waves reach the shore, until trance became stupor. If he sat long enough, following each wave as it rolled forward and broke, bristled and dissolved, he forgot himself, he disappeared, and there was only the water wide across and deep at shore. Tristan liked that feeling. It was not like falling asleep. It was not like dreaming.

Soon the pollen was gone, leaving the water clear fifteen feet to the bottom. Where it was deeper than that, the water was black. Tristan kept his post at shore, watching the waves erase each other. Then one day he jumped in, though not far out or with a cry. He was so small that the hole he broke in the surface closed over his head quickly. Rachel held her breath with him, watching from the slope. He wasn't a strong swimmer yet. There were so many things she needed to teach him. But he wasn't the kind of child who wanted to be taught. Anyway, she thought, you learn for yourself. Which wave would he break through? Which one was he holding out below? When he resurfaced, they could both breathe. She took a breath for his face, one for his neck, one for his shoulders, and one for his chest as he pulled himself out, his skin twice lit by the sun and cold wind. *I love you*, she thought, *my baby*, watching him slip out of the water. His knees were bruised, but he was otherwise perfect, and as if he could hear her thoughts – maybe he could, what did she know – he found her eyes and smiled at her, closed his eyes and seemed to be saying thank you.

Days went by without name for two weeks before a boat came around the front of the island, slowing in a moan of lost momentum. The sound brought Rachel to the window. She knew that she was supposed to go down and help him land. It was the water taxi. It was the same man.

Tristan was playing with cards at the table. His cards were spread out like he was drawing with them, making a landscape: a spade and club forest, heart and diamond sky. She didn't think he knew a card game, and she resolved to teach him one, though she'd never liked cards. She had always preferred doing nothing to playing a game, had never been bored – she was too full of feeling for that. Now she couldn't tell if it was the cards or the man that was making her anxious.

The pines gave shelter and long shade, but Rachel felt like she was crossing an open field as she left the cabin. She was supposed to know there was no protection, no place to hide, but it was something that had to be learned in variation. There's no protection, she told herself, forcing her hands open so she might wave, straightening her back, brushing the hair off her face.

'There's no place to hide,' she said.

He thought about it. 'You're probably right.' On his way, he had imagined that she would take relief in seeing him. That's what people did this far out.

'What do you want?' she asked.

For some reason Rachel's hostility made him comfortable. Maybe because she wasn't pretending anything. Or because no one had spoken to him so directly in a long time. She stood where the water slid up over the rocks, leaving no room for him to imagine coming to shore or getting past her. It was like she was trying to hide the whole island behind her back.

'Why are you smiling like that?' she asked.

Against her will, he made her comfortable too. His face was easy to look at. It had the confidence of someone who lives on the water. He was wearing the same loose clothes as the first day, standing still in the rocking boat.

'I've got something here,' he said, holding out a letter.

When he let go, his fingers stayed bent. He'd worked them too hard, she could tell. She wondered if they hurt him.

'So you're Ransom's daughter?'

He tried to see her father in her face. The scar on her cheek wrapped behind her ear and distracted him. 'You must be his daughter. I saw you in the window up there, and I thought that could be him. I know he's dead and it can't be. I mean, I know it's not, it's you.'

Rachel shook her head like she didn't understand, but she did.

'I knew him.'

'I knew him too,' she said, smiling now. They were familiar to each other.

When she opened the letter a few days later, it was bad but not awful, a couple of pages and a folded map from Codas. He'd heard that she'd taken up camp at her father's fishing cabin. She took the map as an insult: like she didn't know the lake. The letter itself was two pages of small, cloying handwriting. He pressed too hard into the page. Nothing was natural about Codas. It was the longest letter she'd ever received. Did they have a boat? Gas for the boat? Oil to mix with the gas? How would she support herself? Codas told her to come to Treble Island. She should come on Sunday at eleven. If she didn't, he would come the following week to bring them himself.

Sunday at eleven o'clock was when Codas held meetings at his father's old chapel. She'd been to one, about seven years ago, for the memorial of one of the old guys her father used to drink with at the trading post. They'd played the dead man's favourite drinking game: tell a story and, if it's good enough, everybody drinks. The dead man had driven his boat up onto a log boom at night, then tried to walk his way out on the logs and drowned. No one had a story to beat that. Rachel was pretty sure people went to the chapel out of habit, and because they lived so alone and knew they'd find each other there. Were they going to church? Maybe, but there was no service. They might only talk about fishing, or the land claim, or they'd throw a birthday party. Had she thought about winter? Codas asked in the letter. Sometimes people didn't notice the seasons passing. Did she? That wasn't her problem. The seasons never passed with ease. Fall would come first, bright by day, but brutal at night as temperatures fell below zero. People often think they are doing their best, but they are only doing what they want, he said. 'Remember you're not alone,' as if she could forget. 'You have a son.'

§

On paper Prioleau's main channels took the shape of a body falling. A body like a cliff jumper. The legs sunk south, while the arms shot over the shoulders and seemed to be reaching for something. The silhouette was headless. Some people said the lake was reaching for its ghost head. Their island was at the heel of the right leg. Treble Island was mid-breast, its outline a dab shape like a heart. Rachel traced their route on her father's old map. The scale was an inch per mile. From heel to heart, it was six inches, six miles, with two or three miles open to rough water.

On their practice run, the wind had its way with them. Tristan was weak in the bow of the canoe. 'Turn around and watch me,' Rachel said to his back, but he didn't turn around. 'Do you see how I pull on the water? I get ahold of it and pull' – no, he couldn't see – 'and with my top hand I push.' The canoe was moving backwards now; the prow and their bodies were slim, but the wind on the water could make a sail of anything. Tristan dipped his paddle like he was dipping his finger into a bowl of batter. 'Don't lily dip,' Rachel told him. 'Cut in and pull.' He finally looked back, but not at what his mother was trying to teach him; he looked at her dark hair across her forehead, down her shoulders, and at her face which was calm, like she didn't care about what she was saying. But all the more reason that he should listen.

'You're not trying.'

He put his paddle into the lake up to its hilt, but when he pulled back his low hand pinched against the gunnel.

Every day she made him practise, like he was learning an instrument. They went out together, and she knelt him down on a ledge at shore and made him paddle in place, his knees rubbing against the rock.

Tristan's weakness worked its way out of him like an illness. It persisted strangely, disappearing only to claw back in, until it eased imperceptibly, then one day it broke, for reasons of its own, and was gone. That Sunday, Rachel filled the bottom of the canoe with rocks to set it deep in the water against the wind, and they climbed in, setting it deeper. They put their paddles into the water without talking and pressed the canoe into the bay. The bow cut the water so cleanly the cut closed quickly behind them. They drew a disappearing line, which no one saw in the first place: they didn't look back, only down at the sky, pitch-blue in the water, or at the black cliffs hanging over their shoulders. When her top arm grew tired, Rachel told him, 'Switch,' and they slid their paddles over the gunnels and started over.

'I'm keeping note of you, Rachel,' Codas told her when she came to the door to show her face.

'And I of you.'

§

The day was subdued, the sky a locked blue with no clouds. It was the kind of day there was no rush to go out since nothing would change. They woke slowly, talking at long intervals. 'We can paddle to the bottom of the bay and look for driftwood. We'll find good pieces,' Rachel said. Then they were both quiet and she spent a long time combing his hair with her hand. She reached down to where he slept on a thick blanket on the floor.

'Why?' he said.

'I don't know.'

'I'll go with you,' he agreed.

'Okay.'

'What will we do?'

'Have you been bone collecting?'

His hair was getting long and she should cut it, but he looked beautiful and older with long hair curled around his ears and falling roughly at his neck.

'No,' he answered.

'Driftwood's like bones. Not just how it looks, that's obvious. But how it feels. It's so light. We lift our arms and don't feel them, right?'

Tristan didn't know if he ever felt his arms.

'I used to go and collect pieces to keep. I found that one,' she said, pointing above the window to a piece of wood like an open wing. The waves and sand had worked on the wood grain to rib and feather it. There were more pieces above the windows and on the wall behind the woodstove.

Down came the wing. And down came the piece in the shape of a kayak, long and tapered at both ends, with a soft-worn ghost hole in the middle. He couldn't imagine how the hole had formed. Down came the abstract pieces. Animal and human faces. One face had no nose, one face had no mouth. Tristan took the beaver-chew walking sticks at the door and carried them into the woods, where he threw them down, and where, sun-bleached, they spoke out against the dark mottled trunks of the pines. He might have carried two walking sticks at a time, but took only one; two might have touched and rattled as he walked. There were bones in this world, he understood, but he and his mother didn't have to live with them.

She liked how the walking sticks looked the way he'd strewn them in the woods. They set a kind of stage and expectation. She also liked the kayak with the ghost hole overturned in a bank of young ferns. The bird wing was missing. When she asked Tristan where it was, he showed her: he'd pinned it under a rock.

Then two or three days later everything was gone.

'I wonder where the walking sticks are?' Rachel asked.

'I buried them,' he told her.

She would see them later that day, littered across the water, bobbing at shore, looking alive.

The heron's legs were like driftwood sticks, the colour of dust and dry. They'd snap in his hands, he thought. Tristan was frightened of the eye, so he looked at the legs. If he could get his hands on them, he would go ahead and snap them with one sharp bend. He looked at the legs, but when he threw his stone he aimed for the eye.

Rachel didn't want her boy to be a cruel boy. She watched him weigh the stone in his hand but never imagined that he would try to hit the heron.

He missed, but in the same motion was struck in the back by something sharp and hard. Then he was down, chest pressed against the wet rock, face nearly in the water. He stayed down. He knew to stay down without being told.

It was not surprise that Rachel felt as Tristan let go of his stone. It was sadness. And it was sadness she felt as she let go of her own.

'That's what it feels like,' she said, coming down to him. Maybe he could hear her, but he didn't answer.

§

When he talked in his sleep, his small voice strained, like he was trying to sing, but he never sang. She could have reached out then but didn't want to wake him. She had always felt it was embarrassing to be woken from a dream, to know that you were seen when you could not see.

He was dreaming that he was treading water and couldn't find shore. The sky, the land, the lake were all the same fresh black. There was the slightest shimmer, but from what light? He tried to find it from his dugout.

She played shadow to him all day. Only at night could she break off on her own. But here she was leaning over him, her body like a shield, protecting him from what? Maybe she was the reason he never sang out. Maybe she was what he needed her protection from.

She needed him to eat more. Tomorrow he would eat something from a package. They would go to the trading post, and she'd buy him anything. With the money she would get. Her plan was good, because it was not complicated.

Rachel sat on the floor beside him. 'No more of this,' she whispered. She leaned and put her lips close to his cheek. 'No more sleeping on the ground.' He was his own child. She wrapped his blanket around his waist and legs, then pulled her own blanket down off the bed. As she spread it over him, her hands moved across his shoulders, down his arms, to his hands. She wanted to hold his hands down, to reason with him, to tell him to stop talking in his sleep, to stop sleeping on the floor, that he must eat; but then there was a different want, which was to keep her hands off and learn from him.

Dreaming was exhausting. She was grateful to have a night of work ahead. She struck one match and it stayed lit long enough to light the kindling in the stove. There was no question the fire would burn, not smoulder – she'd used all the best pieces. She took her blouse from the old tissue paper it was folded in and put it on, fresh against her skin that smelled strong. She put on her jeans and a loose sweater, pulled her hair back and tied it. When she lowered her chin against the collar of her coat, she could smell the sweet blouse and her body too. As a teenager, Rachel would sell herself to a friend. She didn't think of it as selling sex. They were not good friends, but he would pay her, and they went like that, having sex in his bedroom, even when his parents were home, for about a year until he got a girlfriend. Another time, it was one of her brother Sheridan's friends, who'd heard about what she'd done. He asked her, said he liked her, promised he wouldn't tell Sheridan, and he would pay. At fifteen, she had no other way to get money. She knew those boys, and she wasn't afraid of herself.

She carried the canoe down to the water against her thighs. It felt light, which it wasn't, and so she recognized her body was rising to the occasion. She pushed off and started south, staying close to shore to keep her line. The only place to go at this hour was the drinking house on the mainland at the bottom of the copper-mine road, Sebastian's place. If she was at the heel of the lake, it was at the hip. It was a place only men went, so they would know why she'd come.

An awkward moon lit the way, which seemed right. It would have felt forbidding if the moon had been pretty. It was a useful moon, a hunk like a ham roast, that gave enough light to see the shoreline but roused no wind and called no spirits on.

She passed the time listening to her own breath and the sound of the paddle pulling through the water, and to the eddies that swirled and sucked as she drew the paddle out. After two hours, when she was almost there, she heard a motor. She stopped paddling so whoever it was wouldn't see her paddle flash in the moonlight, the wet blade like a mirror. But it wasn't any use: no one seemed to notice Rachel when she was in plain sight – then they ignored her – but when she tried to hide or slip by, she was cornered.

The boat came straight for her and slowed until the motor idled. It was the water taxi again.

'Is that you? I thought you were a man!' He cut the motor.

She wondered what he was doing out there and decided he was probably drunk.

'Hey,' she said.

'What are you doing out here?'

As she let go of her paddle for the first time, Rachel felt patches of blisters on the palms of her hands. They felt gross, like holding warm teabags. Oh my god, she thought. Paddling back would break the blisters.

'You aren't sleepwalking?'

'I don't think so,' she said, feeling her hands start to pulse.

'Don't tell anyone you saw me out here,' she said.

'I don't talk to people,' he told her.

But that wasn't true, he'd been asking people about her. Why hadn't he seen her before? She had kept to herself, they said, lived outside of town in a trailer with her brother. Now she lived with a boy and had no way to support him. His wife said she'd seen Rachel a few times: 'I don't know what she's thinking. I can usually tell what people are thinking.'

'Are you all right?'

'Yes.' Her eyes were everywhere.

'I can give you a ride where you're going.'

'No, you can't,' she said, 'not tonight.'

She looked out at the water, not at him.

'I'm going to the place up there, Sebastian's,' he told her.

'You are?'

'You should come with me.'

She would have refused and met him later, if that was meant to happen. But her hands.

§

There was no more light inside than out. Over the bar two propane lamps smouldered like abandoned coals, not gold like they should have been, but a sunken red. The brittle mantles were seared at the bottom in black rings. Rachel always wanted to crush dead mantles, since they turned to ash at the lightest touch, into a powder finer than flour. She had to stop herself.

'Where's your boyfriend, Rachel?' asked Sebastian. Women weren't really welcome, but Sebastian had always liked her.

'Oh, he died, I think.' She looked past him.

'He died, you think?'

'He probably didn't die. But if you never see someone again, how alive are they really?'

'Not very,' Sebastian agreed, 'unless you think of them.'

As children they'd danced together, or at least very near to each other, on Treble Island on those summer nights her father kept her by his side. She remembered how Sebastian flicked his fingers as he danced. He would flick them, then pull up and brandish the bottom of his button-down shirt like it was the hem of a dress, showing his stomach then covering it again. He'd shown everyone his stomach.

There were three old guys at the end of the bar, copper miners, she figured by their tight builds and matching black steel-toe boots, and by how they talked so close to each other's faces. They were comfortable that close. They were good at being buried alive together, both under the earth and here, under a cloud of cigarette smoke so thick it looked painted onto the air above their heads, the same grey as their hands and faces.

Summer would bring tourists and migrant workers, but she couldn't wait for them. She was here now, hoping to find a man she'd never seen.

'One day this place will burn down,' said the man from the water taxi. 'It's so dark it's turning in on itself.'

He was right to interrupt her. There was no one else, and she'd already chosen him.

'The dark's good. We can't see how disgusting everything is,' she said. 'The floor, the counter. It's sticky.' She lifted her glass and took a big sip. 'My glass is dirty, I can taste it.'

He looked at her hard.

'Okay, what's your name?' she asked.

'Keb.'

'That's your nickname?'

'No, that's my name. I don't have another one.'

Keb saw that Rachel was too thin. Her bones – her shoulders, the clavicle – pressed against the skin. It was hard to see her whole, since all these lines called for attention. There was her wrist. He'd seen piles of wrists, but never one so clearly. She put her hands on the table and stretched her arms. He followed the movement of her hands from the table to her neck, through her hair, back to the table, down to her thighs. She moved a lot. Only her eyes held still. But she wasn't looking at him. She seemed to be looking nowhere.

He tested himself by staring at her sunken cheek. It didn't make him apprehensive. He told himself that he didn't wonder about the story. He felt defensive on her behalf: her scar wasn't a big deal, didn't make her ugly. It didn't make her hands, or where she put them, less interesting to him.

'You're looking at my face,' she said.

'Yes.'

She didn't mind.

They drank mixed rye straight, and it tasted good until it didn't taste at all.

'I'd go home,' said Rachel, once she realized they'd been drinking for hours. They'd been keeping pace with the miners, but it was impossible to finish with their kind of composure. 'I'd go now,' she said, sliding her legs out against his.

'You can,' he told her.

'I wonder what time it is.'

It grieved him that she should mention time.

Rachel fell asleep in her bed at six-thirty. When she woke at nine she was fully dressed. She smelled of whisky and bile, but her limbs felt light as she lifted them. As she rose she felt exceedingly physically good, better than other mornings. First thing, she took off her blouse and wrapped it in its tissue paper. It was wet at the back – she'd been sweating in her sleep – and crumpled and marked with black down the sides, where Keb had reached under her sweater and put his hands the first time. He'd cleaned his hands on her. But if his hands weren't clean, she didn't blame him. They weren't supposed to be.

She crouched by the woodstove in her bra and held her hands out, but the stove was blunt cold. She filled it with balls of newspaper and kindling and lit it, her hand shaking the match. A strange momentum in her body had carried her out of bed, out of the blouse, to here, and it wanted to keep going, so she put oatmeal and water in the pot, went outside and brought in an armful of firewood. When the oatmeal was done, she filled a bowl and put it down on the table with a hard knock, almost breaking the dish. Distances were hard to judge. Like the distance between her hand and waist. She tried to rest her hand on her hip, but her hand wouldn't land. That's when she remembered Tristan.

She searched everywhere. Under the bed, across the floorboards with her hands. Something was wrong with her hands. She searched in impossible places, as if searching for something smaller than a boy. She opened the cupboards, lifted the blankets, two and three times. Did he always scatter the blankets? She couldn't remember. Maybe he'd been taken away. Someone had come. Her body tightened around the idea. She sat down and threw up.

Rachel rose to her feet, walked wall to wall and touched the walls like a swimmer pushing off. Her hands were beating with pain, a ragged pulse, but she refused to look at them. Her hands didn't matter.

She went to the window, not to look out, but to hate this place she loved. Why did it matter? Why did she think it was hers? She was ready to see the sky empty, the water empty, her eyes empty, but there was Tristan down low on the shore, sitting where he always sat to watch over the water.

'We're going to Treble Island,' she said, coming up behind him, breathing like she'd been running. 'But don't worry, not to see anyone. We're going to the store.'

He didn't look at her.

'You can choose something. I'm going to choose something too.'

'Friends are hard. It's okay you don't have a lot.'

Sitting on the verandah of the trading post, eating butter tarts out of a greasy brown-paper bag, they watched a game of Capture the Flag take place in sprints and chase below. The boys were fast runners, even the smallest ones. Their bodies punched the air as they ran, making room in the crowd and splitting the tall grasses. Their legs wheeled without thought, stopping only when kicked out or wrapped.

Rachel knew these boys were different than Tristan. They were creatures of instinct. They knew exactly what they were doing: this. And later they would do something else. Tristan hadn't said anything since she'd found him at shore that morning. His life, like hers, would never answer any question with that kind of confidence. One boy clipped the legs of another boy. The way people treated her, Rachel didn't think anyone knew what they were doing. They were all making it up – throwing their weight around, hedging against the unknown – and why not just admit that? One boy caught up and pulled another boy's hair, then seemed to apologize, petting him for a long time. Maybe hedging was the answer. Maybe that was what she was supposed to do, hedge, but she never could. Two boys ganged up on a smaller third, but he was explosive and easily outran them, leaving them breathless, hands pulling on the bottoms of their shirts. People disappointed each other but most of all themselves. The two stragglers were livid but still cheerful. One spat hard on the ground at his own feet, as if to say, fuck it, at least we're together and he's alone.

They had to believe in the game. They had to believe in every dash and blow, or get run over. And that's why she couldn't imagine Tristan down there, he was too much a part of her.

He felt her hand on the back of his neck and leaned into it. He didn't know what she was thinking about, but he knew she needed him to be there with her and nowhere else. Together they watched as one boy grabbed the front of another boy's shirt, twisted it in his fist and pulled him to the ground, shoulder first. The shoulder unnaturally compressed and the boy stayed down.

'See, friends are hard.' She would tell him all the hard things.

Time to go, they walked down the boardwalk to the dock with plastic bags full of groceries, the handles stretching thin and banding their skin. The Treble boys didn't make way but included them in their game as obstacles. One boy hid behind Rachel and tempted another to come and get him. Tristan hated that but there was nothing he could do, and soon he was likewise used. The game sped up once they were in it, and now shouts heard as playful from above sounded different – they didn't give direction but menaced – a kind of music like bats flickering around your head. A small fist hit the side of a small head with a pop; a body slipped, another slid; a shoe fell off; a string of beads broke off a wrist, but that was soundless, even the tears. The game was getting better since every second it was more terrible. The point of a stick was dragged lightly down Tristan's back, but he didn't turn. He would fall and hit the ground on that boy's tears, the one who'd lost his bracelet. He'd cover the tears with his chest and cheek, gathering them to himself.

Rachel was satisfied they would make it through the summer as she put her bags into the bottom of the canoe. She liked feeling how heavy they were. It would be an easy trip home with the boat sitting so low.

Tristan saw the flag first, hanging under the front edge of the dock, tied from below. It wasn't a rag like he thought it should be for Capture the Flag, but a fine cloth embroidered at the edge, the wet tip translucent where it hit the water. It shimmered in the strained light under the dock and he liked it.

Rachel crawled into the stern, where finally last night's exhaustion overtook her. Satisfaction brought it on, now that she was done and they had their groceries. Her back ached through to her stomach. The feeling of the canoe's lacquered cedar, warmed in the sun, made her want to lie down. She thought of stretching out in the bottom of the boat. It smelled like a dug-up garden. If the canoe were a cocoon, she would wake in a different shape. She felt herself slipping into that shape already; her chin dropped, shoulders slunk, hands curled around her blisters, and that's when she saw the cloth twisting under the dock.

She thought it was for her. White was her colour. So she untied the tight knot. It was hard to untie, but that only convinced her she was right. It didn't occur to Rachel that a boy might have borrowed one of his mother's kitchen window curtains to make a game worth playing. Later that afternoon, the boy's mother would notice it gone. She wouldn't yell, or even bother to find him, but would sit down and grow quiet because she had saved up for the cloth and had sewn the curtains to please herself, and she never did anything for herself.

§

Keb usually stopped by their place on his way down the lake, but now he wanted to go there straight without an errand. He thought about telling his wife Anuta that he was going fishing, but she would never believe him. You either fished or you didn't. So he told her he was going to work. He was going to put a new roof on the old hunting cabin. Marie could come and hold the ladder, or help carry things. She could play with the boy who lived there.

'Hold the ladder? If you slide over or start to come down, she won't do you any good.'

'She can stretch her legs out.'

Keb had never thought about Marie's legs before this day.

'Marie stays with me,' Anuta told him. Their daughter Marie was going on twelve and Anuta had always kept her close.

'Whatever.' He was going to take Marie.

Keb never came home and wanted to talk. He never woke up and wanted to have sex. He never looked for her anymore in the middle of the day. And now there was this shit.

'She'll like it,' he said, 'so I'll take her.'

'You don't need to take her. Just go and leave her out of it.'

'She'll come. Then I won't be alone.'

'Alone? There's that woman there.'

There was unrest in his pleasure. He dressed slowly, trying to take command of himself.

'You should wear a warmer shirt or put on an undershirt,' Anuta told him.

'This shirt is fine,' he said. It was too thin, night had dropped below zero, but he didn't care.

'You know what, you can take her,' she said. Her only power was to consent. 'But you have to take care of her.'

If she were a boy, Marie would have known how to take the lake – its whole length from heel to throat. She wanted to go out on the water and get sunburnt like her father. His skin was so much darker and more useful than hers; it was rough, it could take the weather. She wanted to be caught in a storm with a wind so strong it would drive them inland to some unfamiliar shore. She didn't know the quality of her father's company, if it was good, but she wanted to know it. Didn't he know that? Every day she ran to the dock, knelt down, untied the ropes to his boat, and flipped them into the hull. 'Watch your fingers,' he sometimes told her. But she did not care about her fingers.

She might have written a note and put it in his pocket: 'Father, please take me with you, away from here and Mother. Mother never smiles at me. She never laughs at anything.' But he would read the note and wonder who'd written it. He didn't notice her, he didn't smile either. She might have written a note like that but never would have signed it. Say she signed it and her mother found out, life would end, but not with a bang. First the clothesline would snap, the clothes would fall and rub into the ground. The ropes holding their boats to the dock would come undone and drag and soften in the water. The generator would cough and stop the water flowing to the kitchen tap. The only alarm would be the doors falling off their hinges and slapping the ground like bodies. Without remark – they never said anything anyway – no one would expect dinner that night or breakfast the following morning. Their cabin would collapse into the heap it was. The lake would rise and swallow their island, taking it back from them. Love, Marie.

She never counted days. Every day was the same day, though it was summer now, so the sun punched a hole in the sky and the heat poured out. She stared at the hole until her eyes hurt, then tried drawing it. But the sun couldn't be drawn; it spread over the water, up the steps, and across the table and the backs of her hands. She tried circles of different sizes. She tried emanating rays, lines stuck out of the circle like candles poking out of a cake. It was with a drudging sense of her own awkwardness that Marie abandoned the sun and turned to her diary. But she had nothing to write down. Nothing until a shotgun fired and echoed in the narrows at the bottom of the bay. It wasn't hunting season. She hoped they missed and wondered if her hope could thwart the shot. She called the sky shot-blue in her mind, then wrote it down, *shot-blue*.

That's when Keb came to the open porch and hit the table she was writing on with a flat hand. He said, 'You're coming with me.'

Marie closed her book and roughly tied back her long, tangled hair. She wanted to braid it but knew this might betray her pleasure and take too long.

Going inside to get her boots, Marie was stopped by her mother. 'You look proud of yourself,' she said. Marie realized she was smiling too much and breathing through her mouth. She had been so surprised by her father and his flat hand that her hands were shaking. She could only stick her boots on and jam the laces in at the top.

'Don't come back a mess!' her mother called after her.

'I won't,' Marie answered, hoping that she might find occasion to make a mess of herself.

As they walked to the boathouse, she didn't look at her father in case he might change his mind.

'I guess you want to know where we're going,' he said.

'No,' she answered, looking straight ahead, 'that's okay.'

Keb didn't know what to think of his daughter. He had always assumed she was like Anuta, since the two of them spent all day together, but it wasn't true. Marie was different. She was unsure of herself. He saw her untied boots and tumbled hair and liked that she was a bit ridiculous. 'I'll sit here?' said Marie, putting her hand on the seat beside him. Keb didn't answer because she could sit anywhere. 'You could use a friend,' was all he said. 'There's a boy your age, just like you.'

The boat picked up and felt light. She'd seen the boy on Treble Island with his mother – she always kept a hand on his shoulder or at the back of his neck. At chapel last Sunday, he'd slept through the whole thing with her fingers in his hair. Marie would have liked to sit with that woman's arm around her, with those long fingers in an arc in her hair.

It was Marie's sin that she longed for a different mother, and maybe that one. 'Stop looking at that woman,' her mother had told her on Sunday. Marie had been staring, it was true. Because they were new. 'Don't stare at her. And while you're at it, don't stare at anything.'

But Marie had kept staring at the woman's back. She was waiting for her to turn. She wanted to see her. The woman's face admitted its own weakness. Marie was sorry, she didn't know what for, but not for staring. Generally she was very sorry, but to no purpose at all that she could understand. Everyone seemed sorry. Or they were angry. This woman was not like that.

Rachel somehow eased Marie's conscience, which was like a pulled muscle, sore to touch. Seeing her made Marie feel that more was possible. For the first time, she started using the word *beautiful* in her mind. That woman's face was beautiful. Something amiss would from then on be a requisite for beauty for Marie. Her face was like the Jordan River in the song Marie loved: *full of waves of sorrow white and high.* The scar was a wave stuck in breaking. It looked awful, like the skin was ground dug up by a dog. Marie wanted to know if it would heal. She didn't want it to, did that make her unkind?

'Such eyes,' she now sometimes said to herself, when there was nothing else to do, lying in bed, feeling the cold air come through the open window; or here, on the water, the waves made sense of the repetition, 'such eyes.' When Marie thought about Rachel's eyes, part of her went gently unconscious. And so it was, Marie, at twelve going on thirteen, was in love with the most unlikely person. She didn't know better, and she would never know better, because she didn't want to.

As they landed on the island Marie realized she had seen nothing go by.

'You stay here. I'll send Tristan to find you,' said Keb.

So his name was Tristan. Marie did not like to tell people her name.

All she knew about this boy was that he belonged to his mother, who kept her hand in his hair. Also, his skin was as white as the inside of a woman's thigh – Marie had overheard Codas complaining about the boy's health to her mother, and that's how he described his pallor. Marie was moved to write it down in her diary that evening. Her mother had answered Codas, 'White as a fish belly-up,' but Marie didn't write that one down because she never wrote down anything her mother told her.

'Why did you bring her here?' asked Rachel.
'I just thought of it.'
'What if she tries to find you and we're together?' she asked, putting her face against his arm. His arms were very long and thin and she liked them. 'You shouldn't have brought her.' She felt close to Keb, not because they were close, but because they were comfortable at a distance.
'She won't do anything.'
'You should wash your shirt,' she said, now lightly holding his hand. 'It smells like gasoline.' She kissed his shirt over his shoulder.
'I'll wash it.'
'You can't use her as cover.'
'I won't.'
Rachel kissed his shirt again. 'Your shirt is disgusting.' She kissed his neck.

Keb wasn't used to affection. He put a hand on her forehead lightly. He looked quickly at her dark eyes, then away at nothing. Her eyes were overpowering, even when she was half-awake.
'Do you know what you're doing here?' she asked.
The room felt like open water. They would drift unless they could decide to go somewhere. Keb wanted to tell her that he loved her but knew it was not the right thing. 'I don't know.'
'I live here,' she said.

Rachel propped plywood boards on the windowsills to block the view. A cut of light still came in at the top and hit the counter, the floor, and the foot of the bed, drawing a line they crossed in and out of. Like this, the cabin reminded her of a clearing in the woods, the kind she could find off-path. She thought about those found places as he took off her clothes and put her down on the edge of the bed. They'd never kissed shyly, only deeply from the start; they fit, and so they could have sex with their full strength, no small thing, their bodies making more and more sense as they used them. He was so much stronger, but Rachel felt his equal. She put her hands on his face, her fingers in his mouth, her hand around the back of his neck. He let her push back, though maybe he had no choice, and when she kicked the headboard half-off by accident, he turned around laughing and kissing and kicked it clean off.

Marie didn't have her hat and suffered for it. The sun was like blown glass turning in a cloudless sky.

Stepping on shore rocks, Tristan approached her. He was a hunter and the boat was a beast. Approaching slowly, he imagined that the long, smooth, varnished boards were covered in thick fur. The heat wasn't coming from the sun, but from the beast's damp breath.

The sun tired her eyes so much she had to close them. This made her feel like an idiot. She sat waiting – for what – and now she would not be able to see it when it arrived.

One day, he would kill this thing and sink the body.

Drugged by the sun, Marie lowered into a bundle on the bottom of the boat.

Tristan started with beady pebbles pulled from the shallows. He lobbed them so high they hung pleasantly in the air before falling. Some ticked against the side of the boat, some fell short in a chorus of tiny sucking sounds, and some shot into the hollow, bounced, rattled.

Three hit Marie, one on the back of her hand at the wrist and two on her neck damp with sweat.

Unaware of the sleeping girl, Tristan tossed a greedy handful that darkened the air like a hatch of flies. A hatch of nails. Marie woke as this cloud descended, covering her head with her hands too late. She whipped her knees to her chest.

Kneeling now in the shallows, Tristan searched the bottom by running his hands over it. What he wanted was to put his hands all over the invading presence. He settled for a stone that fit his palm. The problem with tiny stones was that he could not really aim them. But this one could be controlled. He threw it in a low arch and savoured its flight by tightening his body and holding his breath, listening for a hollow crack. But nothing happened. It never hit. Still breathless – holding it in – he kept listening far past the time it was possible the stone might land.

It mutely struck the side of Marie's small right breast. She was half-blind, her vision mottled by sleep and sun, but she understood what was happening now. As she stood and met him standing alone, up to his waist in the water, she forgot her breast and felt only a near-debilitating rush of sympathy. He looked like a poor little animal, hungry and upset. His face was expressionless, but his bare chest was white and caved in. He was much smaller than she had imagined.

'Hi,' she said.

Tristan tried to run, forgetting that he was standing in the water.

'Hello,' she tried again. Marie didn't know where to begin. Maybe, with Tristan, this was the beginning.

'Are you hurt?' he asked.

'No,' she told him. 'You missed me.'

Rachel pulled Keb's shirt across her chest and went with bare legs to the window. As she took the plywood boards down, she was thinking of Marie. Poor girl, she thought, trying to remember what she looked like. She wasn't sure she'd ever seen her. Tristan would slight her if he found her. Sometimes he slighted his mother.

'Go home,' she said to Keb, still looking out. 'Please go home. I wonder about the kids.'

'No,' he said, not sitting up.

'Yes.'

§

As Rachel and Tristan pulled away from their island early one Sunday morning, the sun rose over their shoulders then sunk back down. The sky lost its grandeur and looked like a bad painting, slopped on. Tristan tried to hide but the rain that came down was so hard it bounced off the lake and came at him from below. 'Don't bother,' Rachel yelled, hating to see him curl his shoulders. She wanted to pull his shoulders back. 'Don't do that, Tristan,' she told him. He was hiding as if he could, but the storm wasn't looking for them – it was oblivious. There was no point in shrinking. She might shrink. She could take any shape, but he must not.

When they landed on Treble, their hands were like wax. They threw their paddles onto the dock and pulled themselves up using their forearms and elbows, afraid to use their fingers. They stood on the dock without talking and tried to let their clothes dry in the wind. But the wind had moved on. Now only small scurrying gusts bristled the skin of the water. As a child, Rachel had believed the wind listened to her, and she would have tried at a time like this to talk to it, but she didn't believe that anymore.

She put her hands under Tristan's shirt, one on his back and one on his chest, but this only made him shake harder. Her hands were cold through the middle. She tried drying his hair with the bottom of her shirt but her shirt was wet.

A few houses stood on the dirt road that led to Codas's land. Laundry snapped in the wind like people clapping, but not in celebration, urging the show to its end. There was a strong sense of expectation that nothing would happen here this morning. Pushing Tristan in front of her to keep him going, Rachel went to the first house. It had a front door the colour of forget-me-nots, those timid flowers that spread like loneliness and took over everything, she thought. They were her favourite flowers.

As she lifted her hand to knock at the familiar blue, two loose dogs sprung out from around the side porch. They barked and jerked, whining high as they spun their tight bodies in circles. They were patchy and pinto, a breed she didn't know and didn't like. If Rachel had been wearing a sword, hung comfortably at her hip, she would have drawn it and slayed them. Instead she walked backwards, pulling Tristan by a handful of his shirt. When they reached the road, the dogs twisted their haunches and bucked like horses, clacking their teeth. That was the blue door.

It was a hard time on Treble Island, so most of the clothes on the lines flew worn, at one with the wind. She looked for children's clothing. Her next choice was a door painted the same brown as the rest of the house. This seemed practical. Before she could knock, the door opened and there stood an older woman with a handsome face and strong body. She was neatly and warmly dressed.

'My name is Rachel and this is Tristan.' Rachel was not feeling well and would have trouble explaining herself.

'I know who you are. Isn't this a small place?'

'I didn't want to bother you.' She was embarrassed that the door had opened before she could knock. 'Do you have something we can borrow? Clothes? They don't need to fit.'

'Clothes should fit,' the woman said. She didn't invite them in but came back with a shirt, pants, and socks. When Rachel reached for them, the woman told her to wait, because she would do it.

Tristan let her. He stood still, held his arms up, lifted his feet one at a time. He watched the woman's unfamiliar, thick hands button his shirt and met her face at the top. She smiled easily and kindly, but also efficiently: soon her smile was done. She was so unlike his mother, who always seemed sad when she helped him get dressed.

Rachel watched with her wax hands stuck at her sides, feeling she would never lift them again. There were no clothes for her.

When they turned to go back to the road, Tristan tried to take one of Rachel's hands, but she wouldn't let him. He tried one side, then ran around her back and tried the other. Rachel pulled her hands out of his reach. This was no protest, she couldn't do it. She felt so tired, like she might lie down on the road there and sleep. It might have been the damp clothes, stuck to her thighs and back, bringing her down in a slow tackle. She tried to think, but couldn't because her body was thinking for her, batting the child's hand.

When they arrived at the old chapel door, Codas was there. What did he think about, standing alone with no one to talk to? she wondered vindictively. He was a poor man with no thoughts of his own. That was poverty. She knew she affected him. Things couldn't be controlled, didn't he know that? People couldn't be controlled.

She raised a tacky grey hand, 'Hey there,' she said.

'Rachel, you look bad.'

'There's no meaning in it.'

Codas had slept through the early storm and had no idea it had rained. It looked to him like Rachel had fallen into the lake. Her hair was wet against a wet shirt. She had to be sick, the boy was dry. But the way the boy was clinging to her, sharing her breath, maybe he would catch her illness, maybe he wanted that.

The chapel smelled like wet ropes and oil and gas. People had come as usual from down the road and paths, and from across the water, to form a small crowd in a land of no crowds. Other than this, Prioleau was clear of human souls.

Rachel's head fell to her shoulder as Codas started talking about the dam schedule.

Tristan didn't know if he should try to wake her.

Sitting a few seats back, Anuta liked the way Rachel's neck looked almost broken as she slept.

Keb wanted to wake her but didn't know how he might.

Codas was not unhappy to see Rachel like this. If things were bad, she would have to come to him.

The woman who had given Tristan the clothes watched him closely. He seemed to have a sense of purpose, standing at his mother's side, protecting her, though he didn't know how and maybe it was impossible. Rachel's head, bent past prayer, was like a flower broken by its own weight. In sympathy, the woman's head started to ache. She should have shared her clothes, she didn't want to punish anyone.

Marie couldn't see Rachel's face, not her eyes. She had no hope of being seen in return. She stared at the rafters to distract from her disappointment. How had they managed to lift those rafters up there? Her mother didn't know anything about rafters. Marie wanted to ask her father, but they didn't know how to talk.

Tristan put his head against his mother's arm. She was asleep, so he tried to fall asleep too. He wanted to sit beside her where she was sitting. He would walk beside her if she were walking. He would wade out if she were in the water. He curled against her like a stray animal.

Rachel caught fever. Her skin stayed damp and her body shook like a small boat tied to a dock in conflicting winds. She could find comfort by moving from the bed to the floor, floor to bed, but it lasted only five minutes before the ropes twisted again; they slacked, sashed, then snapped back so tightly you could walk across them. The dock rings strained. If she were a boat, she would scrape the dock and from the scraping shiver and threaten the only threat she had: to finally break.

Portions of muscle burned away until she felt closer to her core, though also strangely immaterial, shot through with the window light. Her body was always too thin, now it was rugged. She thought her hands looked old and wanted to ask Tristan if he thought so. The bedsheets grew so disgusting she stopped pulling them to her face, worried that if she gave them to Tristan to wash, she'd never see them again. He would spread them in the water and let them fly.

Tristan brought her what she asked for. He made tea from wintergreen leaves gathered on the high side of the island: he boiled the leaves, let the water cool, and picked the leaves out.

He also brought the white cloth, now kept in the closet, neatly folded in the pocket of her winter coat. She still couldn't believe she'd found it. He couldn't believe she'd stolen it. 'Pour some water on it.' He did. 'Twist it.' He squeezed it like a rabbit's neck to take the life out, then handed it over reluctantly. Rachel took it. She wiped her mouth, pressed the cloth to her eyes. 'Go outside.' She was always telling him that.

Tristan left, but his camp was the front steps. He could do anything he wanted. He could fish and cut the fish open with his pocket knife. He could puncture the air sac with the knife tip, let it hiss, then spill the bright black guts out on the rocks and moss, and he did. It made him feel terrible. He hid the guts in the bushes, but they started to rot, it seemed, within an hour. He could smell it from everywhere and had to scrape the guts together and throw them off shore, where seagulls dabbed and picked at the bits that floated.

He stretched out across the steps and pretended to be sick. He pulled a towel over his legs like a sick blanket and rolled his head on the hard board the way she rolled her head on the pillow. Up was the sun. Probably there was sky, but the sun was all he saw, like a breach, like a skinned knee that wouldn't stop bleeding. The sun could be awful, but it was also useful in helping him to suffer on the steps below the door. The sun soaked through the towel, but no matter how hot he was, he would not take the towel off. It was their towel for bathing in the lake, the one they shared, and it smelled like her before she was sick.

§

'Where's your mother?' Keb called from the water.

Tristan heard him but didn't know how to answer.

'Where's your mother?'

'I wouldn't tie my boat up,' Tristan said.

'You don't have a boat.'

Keb had no habit of looking at the boy but now he did, annoyed with his uselessness. Tristan wore wheat boots and kid blue jeans with no belt. The dark blue elastic band of his underwear showed above the top of his jeans, tight around a tight stomach. He had a serious face and tiny body. He was filthy. The skin around his neck was dark and his hands were darker, grimy as if he'd been digging into something, or as if his hands were dug out of the earth. Taking this inventory, Keb was annoyed by a sense of responsibility: someone needed to wash him.

'She's sick and doesn't move.'

'Don't exaggerate,' Keb said, bringing his boat to land and tying up.

Tristan ran over and looked in the bottom of the boat for the girl, but she wasn't there.

Keb absolved himself from caring for Tristan by deciding that he couldn't catch him if he tried. 'Stay and watch my boat,' he said.

Tristan waited until Keb disappeared up the path toward the cabin, then untied the boat and pushed it off.

'It's me,' Keb called out, waiting at the door, not knowing Rachel couldn't get up to let him in.

Tristan had pushed the boat so hard that he almost fell in after it. He wanted to dash the hull on the rocks. He wanted to be the rocks and break the boat with his body. But the boat didn't dash, it drifted and stretched out in the wind and sun and open water. The further it pulled into the clear, the more unsure Tristan felt. He had meant to put something terrible in motion, to answer the question 'Where is your mother?' 'Here she is,' the boat would say, its last words as the rocks ate it up. But he had put something else in motion, something desperate in its mediocrity: the boat gently sailed into the bay.

Keb took off his clothes and got into bed with Rachel, thinking she was only asleep. Her hair looked wet but was drying, he decided. Her skin smelled bad, but he liked her body so much he didn't pull away and would try to get used to it.

Tristan slipped into the water in his underwear and walked out until the bottom dropped off. He swam poorly because he kept looking over his shoulder, back to the island. He knew that he was about to swim out further from shore than ever before.

Where Keb held Rachel, around the lower back and ribs, bruises would appear later in queer shapes like aurora borealis.

The wind was undecided. It carried the boat one way, then the other, spinning it in half circles. Tristan tried to anticipate what the wind would do next, but the harder he judged, the lower his head sank in the water. He took water in his mouth, swallowed some and spat the rest out.

Usually Rachel held Keb's weight off by squeezing her stomach muscles and using her hands to hold up his sides or hips. She didn't have the strength. She could only look out the window for air.

Tristan reached up and grabbed the boat's high side. He was not strong enough to pull himself over, so he hung there, his feet kicking under the slope of the hull. He hung where fish hang on the stringer. He pulled with both arms and kicked the water. But kicking didn't lift him, only rocked the boat down, then away with equal pull.

Keb turned Rachel's head with his hand to see her. He liked the way her hair stuck in dark strips across her forehead. Her mouth didn't taste good, but he didn't care. Rachel half-kissed him back, so loosely it was impossible to tell what was going on with her. He wanted to ask what she was thinking, but that was not a question they asked each other.

Tristan remembered the motor, a war-green Evinrude many times the size of a human head. He needed to take it in his hands. He did. Then he needed to slide his feet on the top plate above the prop where he could stand. He felt with his feet for the plate, found it, and stood. Pulling on the head of the motor, he jumped and threw his upper body over the transom head-first. His stomach caught on the transom lip, then uncaught, somersaulting him into the gaswell. Blood quickly coated the insides of his cheeks, but he smiled in relief.

Rachel's lips were swollen, dehydrated. He kissed her deeply. She was dreaming, and in her dream she was swatting wasps from her mouth, trying not to breathe them in.

Tristan felt around with his fingers. His bottom lip had split against the handle of the metal gas tank. It was nothing, he thought, looking up at the old Evinrude. They were both shining in the sun, the motor in its perfection and Tristan in his wet underwear, satisfied at having failed to drown.

She started to run to the water. There she could shed the wasps like a skin and leave them to dry into empty shells. She would be able to sweep them off the rock in time.

There was nowhere to run, Tristan knew, hunkered in the back corner of the boat like an anchor. There was always this question of running, never an answer.

Rachel made it to the water and dove in, and dove deep, past the top layer, to where the water was colder, but even there her lips pricked and burned.

Tristan's arm was too short to pull the engine's start cord.

Keb came but the feeling was quickly gone, with no wake, and his body stayed tight. Rachel's eyes opened but she blurred and narrowed them to see only his shoulders and chest, not his face. Her dream was done.

The oars clicked into the oarlocks. Since the boat wasn't built to be rowed, it slugged through the water one foot at a time with no glide. Tristan remembered a story his mother once told him about a man who had shot a black bear down in Gaspereau Inlet. He shot it dead but couldn't lift it, not even one of its huge arms off the ground. He'd only thought of killing, not of what comes after. He didn't have the right knife on him to cut through the fur; his knife rubbed and tore, and so the bear was left to rot. Once the water shallowed, Tristan stopped rowing and took one of the oars, stuck it in the bottom rocks and used it for leverage to pull the boat to shore. He jabbed the oar into crevices and twisted to make it stick.

Only when Keb stopped moving did he realize that he was crushing Rachel. Her breath took long, sticky pauses. Her eyes had gone thick. 'Are you crying?' he asked. 'I don't know,' she said.

As he walked down to his boat, Keb still felt tight, and for the first time since they'd met each other, he wondered what would happen to Rachel. She couldn't live on the island through fall, not into winter. He looked southwest, his favourite direction because it was the mouth of the ruling wind, and he tried to tourniquet a building feeling of dread around the question of what he was doing. He thought he'd been taking care of Rachel, but it wasn't true. He promised himself he would never come back. His legs cramped, his knees hurt, and he looked out at the water harder.

Keb saw that the oars had been pulled out of his boat and one was mangled. The promise he had just made to leave and never come back was too new a promise to deter him, so he started back up the path and kept walking until he walked into the cabin without knocking. Rachel was still in bed, the sheets pooled at her waist. What did he think, that she would be up, washing her arms and legs? Sometimes she did that and let him watch.

'Look at this,' he said, holding the oar over her.

'What is that?'

'Nothing,' he said, realizing how ridiculous an excuse it was for coming back. 'Are you okay?'

'Today we're finished,' she said.

'He wrecked this.' Keb put the oar against the wall.

'Who?' She had no idea what he was talking about.

'Why do you act like you're okay?' he said. 'If you're not.'

'Am I acting like I'm okay? I'm not okay, I'm sick as fuck.' She spoke quietly. 'And I'm crying, I think, but I can't tell.'

'You're not crying. You were before.'

'Oh my god,' she said. He was breaking their deal to keep his distance.

'Oh my god, what?' he asked. She had cried through it all and he had never stopped. Never thought of stopping: all he could think of now. She shouldn't have let him do it. She should have stopped him and helped him.

'Your face,' he said. Her scar that was always white was red.

'I don't care about my face,' said Rachel, closing her eyes on new tears. She heard him walk to the counter, where he took back the money he'd put down.

'None of this is helping you,' he said. 'You need to do something else.'

Rachel couldn't get up to stop him from taking the money. She almost said I hate you, but she didn't hate Keb. She only wanted to know why he was standing at the counter and she was lying flat. Why did he get to have those long straight arms and hard lines in his back? Tristan would be strong enough to bring him to the ground, but not yet. He would be able to take the money back. She imagined Tristan as a young man, the powerful feeling of him, and this feeling, his strength, was also hers. She imagined him protecting her, then she passed out and didn't move, not a little, and slept through the afternoon into night.

In her dream huge angels came down and couldn't fit through the door. They had to talk her out of bed to come outside and join them. They had come for her. But if they lifted and carried her, they did not take her all the way, not to where they were going. They put her down at a waiting place. Rachel only knew lakes. She'd never been to the sea. But what else could this be? There was no far shore where they left her. The horizon was so wide she had to turn her head to understand: not where the water ended but where it kept going.

Come with us, the angels said, and Rachel went because they might not ask again. When they abandoned her, she called at their huge backs and at the slopes of their wings. She didn't know their names so she cried for help. She also called her own name, to her own surprise, fearing never to hear it again. But why would they answer calls of her name? Maybe it was that kind of stupidity that had made them abandon her in the first place. Rachel didn't know what she had done wrong. Everything she knew was useless. It had always been useless, now it was more. For having briefly known them, she was more alone. One had held her hand on the way out, which was also the way in, and now her hand was empty, aching in a way she'd never known it capable of. It was strange, because she didn't want the aching to stop. Rachel was afraid, but she would stay and wait in case they circled back. She wanted to see them again and confirm the ache in her hand. And when she woke finally, two days later, it was with such reluctance that she was not completely there. She was still holding watch. She was, she guessed, at sea.

§

Over the next two months, she tried to keep their routines going. It was obvious to those who saw her on the lake or at the trading post that she wasn't feeling well. She seemed to have trouble hearing. Tristan knew it was hard for her to get dressed in the morning. She would pick up and drop her clothes. She would have to sit down and pull them on. It became the only thing he could see when he looked at her: how hard she was trying.

In October, winds from the north subdued the pines, slowed their sap to a drip. Frost took the knees out of the ground life. Sometimes there was a southern wind that rustled the ground and made it look alive, but only in passing before the cold took back everything it owned. There were warm afternoons that felt endless, but then they ended: a trick of the senses in the headrush of decay.

In late October, after the first heavy snow, Keb took his family to town, to a small house they kept there for winter's harshest months. The lake was freezing up at shore, and in sheets in the calmest coves, but the ice would quickly spread, closing the open water. If they were going, they needed to get out.

The day his boat went by, packed high over the gunnels, Rachel asked Tristan to help her pack the canoe. His mother slept as he threw their clean and dirty clothes into a garbage bag. He had to wake her to roll up the bedding, and together they put that into another bag, tying the top tight against dirty weather out on the water. When Rachel wasn't looking, he took her mirror off the windowsill, wrapped it in a tea towel, and put it in his inside coat pocket, where it would sit, hard against his chest – it could have stabbed him – for hours as they paddled through a light snow. The snow fell white against the black water, and white and grey through the pines on shore.

He was strong in the bow. He needed to be, though he couldn't feel his hands, his fingers as red and white as a Red Devil lure from the wind's lash.

So they ended up on Treble Island after all, on the chapel grounds, living in the outbuilding, no more than a shed with a woodstove. Rachel didn't have anywhere else to go, or money to get there. Bringing her a box of supplies and speaking with her politely, arranging for a delivery of firewood to her door, Codas thought Rachel understood him finally, which she didn't; she had never tried to understand him. She understood only that winter was unthinking. She understood they'd grown low on supplies and that the water at shore where Tristan drew his buckets full would freeze early and stay frozen. The cabin door had already frozen shut one day, and they couldn't open it until the afternoon sun beat relentlessly against it. Only the sun had the secret knock.

The chapel shed had a simple metal bed and a potbelly stove that in the dim light looked like a black dog hunkered in the corner. Everything was in reaching distance: from bed you could reach out and touch the stove and table. Sitting at the table, you were sitting on the bed. There was an oil lamp with a tall glass shell and a reservoir of yellow liquid at the base. At the foot of the bed there was a tin basin for washing dishes, where you also washed your hands and face.

Tristan felt anxious trying to sleep, his skin dry against the sheet. The winter air was so dry it tightened everything. The lake tightened to ice, and the water flowing from the eaves and branches tightened into icicles that broke in the wind. It was hard for him to breathe deeply. Sometimes he felt it most first thing in the morning, when least expected: a shortness of breath. Maybe it was the woodstove burning, eating up the air.

Tristan liked to open the woodstove door to watch the fire. His mother sometimes let him, but other times without a word she would get up, come over, and close it. The darkness suited her. She felt she wore it around her shoulders. When she went out, Tristan would open the door until the hinge pinched. Sometimes he lit the oil lamp too, not to see, just to watch the flame, which he thought of as a knot of wind he might untie by staring at it. They had to burn the oil carefully, slowly and low, his mother told him, because it cost them. But he couldn't help it. She would go out and he would raise the flame until it lashed and blackened the sides of the glass tube. There was guilt at that, but the worse he felt, the more he needed the light.

§

During freeze-up Keb was in town and couldn't see Rachel, not even at a distance in the crowd of Sunday. He sometimes went to the Hotel and Bait and pretended to wait for her, drinking pitchers of beer to himself. He pretended to wait until he felt sick with disappointment and relief. All his feelings, good and bad, were precipitous and he followed them down. He outdrank himself, and when that didn't bring any calm, he picked fights with his friends to get out of his head. He fought to feel less alone. If he ever felt content, he didn't trust it because it had no origin.

Looking out had been his posture, but now he wandered inward to a weaker bearing. He didn't know what do to there. He could only half look at himself in furtive glances, so he was stuck with first impressions. He could not stop thinking of Rachel. He couldn't remember what he used to think about before he knew her. What did he used to do? He had no idea. She would find another lover. She was the least sentimental person he'd ever met. She would never feel sorry for him and he hated her for that. Of course he didn't hate her, because he loved her, but she would never come here when he was pretending to be waiting.

In late January, he was called to the icefields. A few men were needed to clear an island. In summer Keb was the lake's taxi and freight boat. In winter he was someone you called if you needed an extra man to survey land, haul materials, or tear shit down. Clearing land, you worked all day into lightfall with disregard for how you felt. You had to put yourself in ignorance of yourself; if your legs grew too tired to pick up your feet, then you used your back and stomach muscles to lift the dead weight and throw your legs forward like bags of cement. All you heard was your own breath, and you held on to its plain rhythm like a song because you needed it. The final feeling was dried salt, grit accumulated around your lips. You felt and tasted that for a few seconds in bed before passing out. When Keb worked at clearing the land, he was too tired to want Rachel. By day, work was all; at night, sleep. He felt he could think more clearly, because he wasn't thinking.

He was sent off the island one day and could have protested to save himself, but he didn't. He took one of the snowmobiles to the trading post to buy supplies for the camp. There was a light fresh snow, so the ride was fast, which made him feel more powerful than he was. He walked past the store, to the chapel, past that, and onto the open field that led to the shed. There were no footprints, which meant they hadn't come outside today.

As Rachel opened the door, he looked at her neck, not her face. He didn't say hi. Somewhere in the middle of the field, he had decided not to leave time or space for any special feeling or new understanding. He would tell her what she needed to know, then he would leave her there.

'You should know something,' he said.

'Something?' she asked, standing forward in the door, not letting him in. 'Tell me what it is.'

But he didn't want to tell her now.

'Keb,' she said. Moments of silence with him had never led to anything interesting.

'Men have come with contracts to your land.' He spoke almost in disbelief, easing his way into it. 'I think Codas put them onto it.'

'They're liars then,' she said. 'I have papers. They're in the bottom of my clothes chest.' She didn't have any papers. She didn't have a clothes chest. But it was her land. 'That island's my father's.'

'He's been gone a long time.'

'What are you saying?'

'They're clearing the trees,' he said.

'When?'

'They're gone from the front. I've seen the plans. They have a sheet of paper as tall as a man and they unfold it on a table.'

Rachel's hands fell at her sides, surprising her. They felt like something she was carrying and needed to put down right now. She laughed at how they felt.

'Why are you laughing?'

'I'm not.' She couldn't explain.

'You're laughing at me.'

'I'm not.'

'The trees collapse. You cut in and the base snaps because it's frozen.'

'I don't care.'

'They all came down and we slid them over the snow, pulling them with snowmobiles.'

'What about our cabin?'

'They burned it to make room.'

'Room for what?'

He didn't know.

'How do you know?'

'I was there.'

'You helped them?'

'I was working for pay. I wasn't helping anyone.'

'You son of a bitch,' she said, trying to feel angry, but all she felt was tired. The veins in her arms felt like vales. Ice air off the chapel field was blowing through her into the shed. In a way, she liked it, how she felt; it was a new feeling and it had been a long time since she'd given up the idea of new feelings. Maybe she would have new feelings she never expected, but no use for them. 'You son of a bitch,' she said, repeating it, unable to make it satisfying. It was like trying to remember the lyrics to a song, but it had been a long time and the melody wasn't right.

'I have to take any work I can get.'

'Me too,' she said, laughing at him now.

'They're going to pave a tennis court there.'

Rachel shut the door behind her. Tristan was close at the table and she didn't want him to hear.

'Do you think they'll let you play?' Her voice turned intimate.

'Tennis? I don't care.'

'You can't play tennis in those shoes.'

Keb looked at his boots. They'd lost their proper shape a long time ago. He had never thought his boots meant anything. 'I wear these every day.'

'I know.'

'I don't want to play tennis,' he said. 'I don't play games.'

'You'll build cabins they'll never let you in. They'll ask you to come over to fix their boats and shit. They'll talk to you through the screen door.'

'I don't want in,' he said. There were so many things she thought about that he never did. 'What makes you think I care?'

'You would care if they were on your land.'

'It's not your land anymore.'

'Yes, it is.'

'Your father was a squatter, Rachel. He never owned anything.'

'I don't care what you think.'

'You're right. It doesn't matter what I think. When I was taking the trees down, it didn't matter what I was thinking.'

'Did you think of me when you burned the cabin?'

'Yes.'

'I hate that.'

'When can I see you?' he said.

'What do you mean?'

'I don't feel good about you here. This is not okay. You shouldn't live here.'

'You don't feel good? Do you know what I feel?'

'No,' he said.

'Me neither.'

'You should go inside. You're not wearing anything.'

'I'll see you later,' she said.

'When?'

'That's not what I meant.'

Without looking at Tristan, Rachel put her coat on and went outside. Tristan would understand that she needed to be alone. She was seduced by exhaustion and wanted to feel it more. It made her neck loose and head light. She wanted to feel everything as deeply as possible. And she did – with each step in the snow, then drawing her legs out. All was white around her, no matter what colour it was. Coated with snow wind-burnt to ice, the black trees reflected the sun so intensely they shone like mirrors. She walked among them into the white, which was also silver, away from the chapel grounds, the road, the row houses.

She walked off every path she came across into the woods, moving not by sight but by hand – lunging, grabbing at branches to pull herself forward. Low in the underbrush, she could feel the forest's dormant life. An underworld packed beneath the snow: plants and animals playing dead, a flood of them holding on to the smallest heat, in no rush to rise again. The confidence of this sleeping world radiated a gravity she could feel. Her thighs felt heavy, her ankles weak, her feet numb. Snow packed into the cuffs of her shirt and melted down her sleeves. Her hands hurt – but her hands were hers to run across the shells of snowbanks to nurse and ice them, which she did, only making them worse.

It was hard to tell if she was feeling more or less. Her hands said that when you open the body, it spreads red, also clear. If she didn't look, it was nothing. Blood was put on. It was something people did. People did everything to themselves, and to each other, and never admitted it, she thought. She was doing something to herself but didn't know what – she knew not to lie down, and didn't lie down. She didn't fall either, but sank onto her side, folding her hands across her chest to put them away. Then she half buried herself like a sled dog, feeling the acquisitive cold, knowing she had only her body to give up.

When she woke, night was past black into silver. There was a tinct of moonlight on the frozen trees, and she pitied them for being lit when they might sleep. Poised, hovering, they had no choice. They too would fall and sink into the forest floor, just not yet. Sleep had made her more tired, if that was possible. Her body felt like a heavy coat, cut out of thick leather, too big for her, stiff in the shoulders. Her body felt like a big man's coat. She tried to take it off, but she couldn't raise her arms, stuck at her chest. Her fingers were so cold she couldn't bend them, like the branches of these trees. Afraid her fingers might break, she didn't touch them to each other. She wanted to cover her face with her hands. There was a violence to her wakefulness: another new feeling. She had fallen asleep, was gone, then thrust back – into the silver trees, as if they were leaning down to her, which they seemed to be. They might break, she thought, shatter like mirrors, and maybe she was becoming one of them, first the hands.

Sleep was something she would never understand. The simplest things were the most complicated. She didn't know what she was doing here, sleeping and thinking about nothing. Her mind started to race and fall through the underbrush. She stood to try to catch up, but was very slow to run, which made her think of Tristan. He was a slow runner. Lately he was reluctant when she tried to get close to him. He would have been afraid of her right now, of the way she was carrying her hands in her arms. Maybe she would have been afraid of him, how she loved him. But he rarely spoke. It was unkind, she felt, even for a boy.

She moved out of the trees onto the snowdrifts of the flat east shore. The east was all small coves, half-sheltered from the wind that funneled down the channel. Rachel knew that if she tried walking back through the woods, she would never make it home. She had to cross the ice, cove by cove, or go far out and come around wide. She moved from land to ice without noticing the threshold. Her body couldn't keep up to where she thought she was. It felt like she was running ahead, but she wasn't running; she was sliding a little at a time, half slipping back. When she fell, she couldn't use her hands to break her fall. She banged her knees hard, waited for them to hurt, but felt nothing. She felt no pain, only doubt. She doubted her knees, doubted her hands. It was more than thirty below, probably, but she didn't feel the cold; she felt her body like a coat growing heavier, weighing her down. She carried the coat on her back more than she wore it. A few steps across the second cove, she collapsed under its weight, and it held her there in place.

She stood and fell again, hands battered underneath. Her face took the brunt of the ice this time and she stayed down, lifting her head to keep her eyes fixed on the point of shore she was aiming for. She thought she was walking there. Maybe she was half running, maybe she was down. She told herself to hurry, to breathe again, and took quick breaths like the quick steps she was walking in thought. The cold air came in with these breaths and rimed her lungs. She started swallowing, trying to swallow the air all around, to catch it between her teeth. She bit at the air, that was the last thing. Before she died, she did not imagine dying.

Tristan felt the thinness of the shed walls. He was waiting for her footsteps, for the door. He lay on the bed with his face to the boards, listening. Now and then he banged his knee to make a noise to check his hearing. He put the palm of his hand against the wall and it was cold, the fire was low. Queasy with unhappiness, he pulled his hand back and covered his mouth. Where should he go? Where she had gone. First he would run through the field. The tall grasses that in summer swelled around your legs and made it feel like you were running in water, these grasses were crushed and buried under. He would run faster than ever. He went to the table and felt for the small box of matches, found it, shook a match out, and lit the oil lamp. He drew out the wick to make a long blue flame. What if she came home now and caught him wasting the oil? Then he would be caught. He would tell her he always lit the lamp when she was away.

Morning came and he crossed the field. It had been such a bitter night the snow on the ground was hardened to ice and he was able to slide over it, half skating on one foot, using the other to push and drag for balance. Far below the chapel, small fishing huts dotted the bay. Trampled-down paths between the huts made lines, strange patterns in the snow that he liked and followed with his eyes. There were dead ends where huts had been pulled away. There were straight lines, arches, all drawn by the routine of the fishermen checking on each other. It was beautiful and made Tristan forget the night. He had to ask himself why he was there, what he was looking for.

Mr. Matthews was an old man who liked to work alone despite the protests raised by his sons and friends. When he was young, people had questioned his solitary days on the ice and on the open water in summer, but he had never answered them. Time was unpredictable when people were with him: it could go by too quickly, or be an obstacle, obdurate as hell, and not an interesting hell. Alone he felt at peace. So he surprised not only Tristan but himself by stepping out of his hut into the boy's path.

'Come in here and sit down with me,' he said. Mr. Matthews never changed his voice to talk to children. He spoke loudly, just like he was talking to another man.

Tristan tried to keep walking, but the man said again, 'Come in here.' Tristan did what he was told, ducked into the small dark room and sat down on the ice floor.

'I've seen you walking around,' said the man. 'I've seen you all morning. I don't know why anyone wants to walk around like that.'

Tristan didn't know what to say.

'At least don't sit down there, sit on the bench.'

Tristan didn't feel like he could stand up again.

Mr. Matthews saw what was happening, went over and lifted the boy onto the bench. 'You're like a little animal,' he said, happy to discover that he had not ruined his own peace. 'You can sit here beside me.'

The warmth of the hut, the quiet and sudden calm, meant Tristan soon fell asleep, collapsing against the stranger.

Mr. Matthews missed hits on his lines. He could see them being tapped – the fish taking the bait then spitting it out. Some of the hooks were probably stripped, his bait lost, but he couldn't check because he didn't want to let the boy's head drop down. His head seemed to weigh nothing, like a leaf that could catch a breath of wind and blow off. There was something heavy in the boy too, but not his body, which seemed weightless, like a spirit's or angel's. He could be that. It was not the kind of body you let fall.

When the sun started to set, Mr. Matthews used his hand to hold up Tristan's head, then he woke him by saying, 'Okay.' He only had to say it one time.

Tristan didn't walk to shore. He ran all the way to the shed door, and ran up against it. When he found that Rachel still wasn't home, he lit the woodstove, then he lit the oil lamp and sat down in front of it.

Over the next days, Tristan did the same thing. Some of the other fishermen befriended him, but they were not like Mr. Matthews. They teased and played tricks. They handed him their lines but taught him to set the hook too hard, so it pulled out of the fish's mouth or tore and gaped the lip. They made it seem like tying the knot to bind the hook to the swivel was mysterious. He lost many hooks and was told to pay for them by running errands. The men made him run for tobacco and rolling papers, firewood, and even pinecones. But that was just one more of their jokes: burning pinecones smelled like pussy, ha ha ha.

Mr. Matthews told Tristan what he needed to know but made no project out of him. For the most part, they sat together in silence, how they liked.

'A fishing line is like a string of hair,' Mr. Matthews said. 'You can't tie it too tight and you can't yank it.' Pulling huge trout out of the slush, one by one, Tristan could feel the line stretch.

After a week he ran out of supplies and had only their Christmas tins of flour and sugar, and some dried beans, rice and salt. He traced the cursive pink on the tin with his finger, *Merry Christmas*, and cooked a kind of tasteless bannock on the woodstove. He burnt it to make it taste like something. Then the flour ran out and he started following Mr. Matthews home.

Mr. and Mrs. Matthews didn't question the boy, because he was a boy. His mother was not taking care of him, or couldn't, but that wasn't special. Mr. Matthews thought the wicked, so often talked of, were hard to find. There were no people like that. So they asked no questions of the kid, only began to expect his company, appreciating his cautious way of coming and going. He didn't speak, but sat close by. He was otherworldly with his long hair that needed to be cut, his clothes that needed to be washed, his unrevealing eyes. He didn't smell good. Mr. Matthews thought of Tristan as a spirit animal, a gift but not to own, a messenger maybe. He let him operate on his own terms.

The woodstove drew fast in forty to fifty below. By the time Tristan got back to the shed at night, the morning stoke was burned to ash, no coals. He went to bed fully dressed, with his boots on and thick blankets tucked around his neck or pulled over his face. He pulled the blankets up for warmth, and so he could smell her. Until his mother was gone, he didn't know that she smelled like this, a certain way. She smelled like cedar, he thought, but not fresh-cut. It was cedar on the ground, warm in the sun, starting to decay.

She had disappeared into dry air. She must have crossed the ice, they said. She must have headed to town or jumped the train line. The boy was the child of a child – he was hers – with the same thick black hair and vague mouth. He looked just like her. At morning, he waited out on the open ice. Mr. Matthews had to remember to call him in. If he didn't, he was sure Tristan would have stood still until he fell.

If he annoyed people, they couldn't say why. If he saddened them, he didn't look sad himself. He tried to ignore how the snow was turning to slush on the paths. The snow was supposed to hold on to the roof of the shed, to the eaves and sills of the row houses; it was supposed to climb the base of the trees and silhouette the branches. The snow had held on with teeth like the tiny tight teeth of the bass you grab to land and that rough your thumb. The snow had held on but was letting go now: it melted, dripped down and wet his hair. The walls of the shed were wet inside and out. The men pulled their ice-fishing huts to shore, and a week later the ice went out in a way no one could ignore. It moaned through the night like someone was sick in the family.

This was the real new year on Prioleau Lake, time for resolutions. The smell of the earth returned and made more seem possible. And in this spirit, Codas told Mrs. Matthews, 'On the next boat, he goes.'

Codas didn't have to explain who he was talking about.

'No.'

'We have to do the right thing.'

Mr. Matthews didn't know what that meant. 'Where will he go?'

'I have no idea.'

'I beg your pardon?'

'I don't know, but we can't keep him here. Rachel must have gone down south, so he'll go south. He should follow her.'

No one wanted what happened next, not even Keb, and he was the one who did it. He was stuck in town for breakup. For weeks the lake was covered in cankered ice, open only in patches, a gasping black. He was going to Treble Island. He didn't have to explain. 'I'm going down the lake today,' he told Anuta at breakfast.

She didn't answer, but Marie couldn't help herself. 'Find out if it's really happening,' she said. There was a rumour Rachel had disappeared.

'Happening?' Anuta said. 'It already happened.'

More than once Keb had wished Rachel gone. He told himself that he wished it because of the money he gave her. But that wasn't it. By picking up extra work, he had paid for her easily. And he didn't care about money anyway. He didn't care if people knew they were together. If he seemed complicated to people, he was. He had wished her gone because of her: her ambivalence.

'Don't we know each other?' He couldn't stop remembering this. 'We try, I guess,' she'd said. 'Why don't you try harder?' 'I don't want to.' Her answer.

She was gone, the grocer told him. Keb couldn't remember the grocer's name then, though he'd known him his whole life. Standing in the cereal aisle, he felt that his heart was something loose in his jacket pocket, a folded square of paper, dry and tricky to slip out with his fingers. He tried to be gentle, not to crumple the paper as he picked it out and unfolded the creases. He felt his heart was a list and it would tell him what to do next. But he did not have his heart in hand. It was a list of groceries Anuta had given him.

Keb went home from the grocery store, walked through the door straight into the living room and sat down in a chair. It was Marie's chair. It was too small for him still wearing his winter parka. He sat there and began to sweat, feeling sorry for himself, and also embarrassed by the sweat. He needed to get up, to change his clothes, to put water on his chest, to wash his face. Instead, from her chair, he played fourteen games of gin rummy with Marie. He liked Marie's company. Everyone should be like Marie, he kept thinking, including himself. Marie let him sit in her chair. She didn't ask him why he was wearing his coat.

'It's not a sure thing,' Codas told Keb. 'There's no body.'

'Think she took off?'

'People say she could've walked out, but no one has before.'

It made Keb sick to think of someone finding her. He'd been possessive but now was more so. He should go home, he thought. Instead, he walked past Codas and continued to walk through the field behind the chapel.

Before he could knock, Tristan opened the door and put his head out.

'Let's see you,' Keb said, pulling the boy outside into the damp air, though he was wearing only a T-shirt and underwear. He'd been running the stove all morning and had made a sauna of the shed. Tristan started shivering and tried to step back inside, but Keb put his hands on him. 'Spin around and let me see you,' he said. Tristan didn't move, only looked at Keb. His eyes were too placid for a boy, and so was his voice. 'Why should I spin around?' he asked. He didn't want to spin.

§

The cushion Tristan sat on in the bow was warm from the sun and gave him a dim impression of breath and life in the hollow of Keb's boat. He told himself it was nothing. He told himself it was a boat, not the beast he'd stoned and stoned and never killed. He might have asked where they were going, but put his head down instead and closed his eyes. When he opened them some time later, familiar coves and cliffs stretched out around him and rose high. He was headed home to their island.

He used to pass these cliffs in the canoe, looking hard at the cedars growing out of the rock slough that couldn't be enough to nourish them. 'Not enough dirt to cover your tongue,' his mother had said, he remembered. It had been his habit to look through the first rows of the trees into the darkness behind to search for animals, their movement or shapes, and when he couldn't find any animals, he would lean over the gunnel and let his ribs rest against it, and he would look down at the mute bottom rocks sliding under the canoe. They shape-shifted as the boat cut across them. But not today. Today the boat clove the water and with its easy speed clove him from these old feelings.

They pulled up to a long finger dock at the back of the island. The dock was new, the wood so freshly cut it glowed. 'You'll work here for food and a place,' Keb told him as they pulled up.

Tristan didn't understand. At the end of the dock, there was a path where there had been no path the year before. It was cut wide enough for them to walk side by side, but Tristan didn't want to walk beside Keb. He'd never been with anyone on the back of the island.

These were his trees lying down. His to brush past and lean on. Their song was so huge he could never hear it all. Now he walked past and over their stumps. One stump smelled more sweetly of pine than the whole island ever had, and Tristan breathed it in and hated how sweet it was, and wondered how the smell of something dead could be so appealing. The stumps were sticky. Sap pushed up through the cuts, sent by roots below to what was now a bad dream of branches. Did the roots not know the tree was dead? Tristan rubbed his hand in the sap and his fingers stuck together, then burned as he tried to stretch them open.

The path ended in a clearing where their cabin had been. Keb walked Tristan around to show him. 'They need workers here. You can work for them,' he said. 'They're building a lodge, sleeping cabins, docks, and whatever they want.'

Tristan searched the ground for a sign they'd lived here. He searched thoroughly, wanting to fall to his knees and use his hands. But he didn't fall as three men arrived on the far side of the clearing, walking down another new path.

'Keb, good to see you,' said the first man.

It was Richter, leading the others. His clothes were clean and his hair was cut in a style Tristan had never seen, parted on a white line down the side. He had short bangs on his forehead, which he kept brushing away as if they were in his eyes, though they weren't.

'We've missed you,' Richter told Keb.

'I would've sent word I was coming today, but I'm the one who sends word. So here I am.'

'Okay.'

'I brought you a set of hands from Treble Island. They're small but good.' He pushed Tristan forward.

Richter thought the kid looked bad.

'Tristan, shake his hand,' Keb said.

Tristan did what he was told. He put out a sticky hand.

'You can tell him what to do,' Keb went on. 'You can't always tell a man that.'

Richter and the others guessed Tristan's age in their heads. He was ten, eleven, twelve at most.

'How old are you?' Richter asked Tristan.

'Thirteen,' said Keb. He didn't know that Tristan was eleven. He'd never known his age.

'Thirteen years old?' said Richter.

'It was a long winter, he'll fill out. He's got a good look to him, you'll see.'

Richter looked, and thought Keb might be right. The boy's face defied time. He was pale but had the blackest eyes and the most unusual rich black hair, features that spoke to inner resources. 'I think I might see what you mean,' Richter agreed.

'Tristan, Mr. Richter owns this island.' Keb made sure Tristan understood what was happening to him.

'We're going to make something out of it,' said Richter.

This was his mother's land. Tristan would tell them.

'He's a good boy.'

'You'll look after him?'

'It's not like that,' said Keb. 'He looks after himself.'

Tristan stopped listening and looked at the ground. He could see rake marks in the dirt. He would come at night and run his fingers through the furrows to see if anything could be found.

'Do you know the waters?' he heard twice.

There's one water, Tristan thought.

'He's not from this arm of the lake,' said Keb, stepping in, 'but I'll teach him.'

Why only burn their house? He would burn down the whole island and rake it all. He had to make sure not to burn the rake. Then what would they think of him? They wouldn't say he wasn't from here. They would say he was Rachel's son, and that's why he had done it to them, and that's why he had done it to himself.

BOOK TWO

'Learn how to turn your face.' Tristan was already learning. 'Like this,' said Keb, turning the boy's head for him, his fingers roughly in his hair.

Tristan closed his eyes and let his head turn.

'Don't stare at people. Look here – ' said Keb, pointing below his own shoulder, just over the breastbone.

'Where?' Tristan opened his eyes a little.

'Look at the neck.'

He looked at Keb's neck. It was sun-soaked, burnt in the creases.

'What's there?'

'Nothing. Look there and you're not staring.'

Keb wondered why he was doing this. The workday was nearly over. And the boy's hair was the same as Rachel's. It was almost black, like rain-soaked tree bark. Putting his hands in Rachel's hair had been like rinsing them over the side of the boat. They disappeared. He had to pull back.

Two years of cutting and clearing, pounding and ratcheting, and lifting walls and roof trusses had turned Tristan's island from an island like any other, a covered place, into the most open on the lake. That's how they wanted it. Trees fell without ceremony. The more that fell, the more sweet they smelled, Tristan thought – so sweet he gagged and held his breath walking by.

No one knew when his birthday came. He didn't say anything, turning twelve with hands and arms burning, carrying buckets of cement from the mixer to the holes, helping to pour concrete footings for the lodge and its constellation of small cabins on the hill behind; turning thirteen the day a generator as tall and wide as a man with his arms outstretched was hauled in on a barge. They wrapped chains around the generator, bound winches to trees, and winched it up the cliff, scraping a swath of the cliff clear of its pale green lichen. They set the generator down behind the lodge to power electric lights. It was silent that day. But its damp roar would soon grow more familiar to Tristan than the wind in the far islands.

He was sent into the trees by Keb to tack up the black-coated wire flowing from the generator, one tree to the next. He was told to hammer the tacks at the favourite height, he knew, of small birds to build their nests. Tristan imagined the wire was a black snake eating up all the bird eggs. It snaked from the lodge to the fishing docks, then east to the gravel tennis court, where he and Keb hung a cluster of bulbs under black metal hoods.

All clusters in trees threatened to come down: birds migrating, bats on the hang, caterpillar tents splitting. So these lights above the tennis court threatened, swinging in the wind, flickering as they killed insects, hissing and humming a dirge over the more subtle song of the wind and waves. They were hateful to him. The island was supposed to fall into darkness. Then he could smell the ground's decay, the resin of the trees, like the smell of blood when he was cleaning a fish and the blood poured out across the wood.

In the dark, it was easy to imagine it wasn't now: none of this had happened. In the dark it could be three years ago, or one hundred years. In the dark he was himself before. To imagine it, he had to wait until they turned the generator off for the night and the lights coughed out. He had to outwait them, let them go to bed and fall asleep – without falling asleep himself, keeping watch on the rocks below their old cabin, though the cabin wasn't there anymore, not even a piece buried under the lodge with its gaping double door.

Her mother tried to show her how to pack a suitcase, but Tomasin didn't want to imagine where she was going or what she might need there. She held her hands out at her shoulders, forming a cross.

'What are you doing?'

'I'm stretching.'

'What are you stretching? What muscle? I've never seen that stretch.'

'My body,' Tomasin said.

'Fold this.'

Tomasin watched as her mother hung a shirt over the right arm of her cross. Blood moves – it skirts – she could feel it. But her blood didn't just shuffle along as she breathed out, trying to slip the shirt off her arm and onto the ground by force of will. Her blood rushed insurgent from her heart in a current all its own. It was a river that pulled her under and through its rapids and lulls. This was, by now – she was sixteen and had never felt different for a day – familiar. The shirt fell.

'Why are you standing like that?' her mother asked.

'You have to hold stretches for a long time or they don't work.'

'You'll need that shirt.'

'Who can tell what I'll need.'

At the train station, her mother began to cry.

'Don't be sad. I'm the one who should be sad. You're putting me on a train.'

'By the end of summer you'll have money to spend, and it's so hot here, Tomasin, no one likes it.'

'I like it.'

'You'll be on the water. You'll like that.'

'You don't know what I like.'

'You don't know what you like either,' her mother told her.

'Do you know what you like?' Tomasin asked back.

'Some things, I do. And I know what I don't like.'

When the train arrived, Tomasin didn't hesitate. 'Here I go,' she said.

Her mother tried to touch hands but missed, and couldn't tell if Tomasin had pulled her hand away.

Ten hours later Tomasin stood on a pool of loose gravel, the platform of Prioleau Station. The racket of the train all day had been a constant comfort, at least a distraction, and now she felt abandoned to her own thoughts, and while some people liked nothing more, she liked nothing less. A small crowd gathered to meet the train, and when the crowd grew to the size of a class, she felt better, commotioned. Look at me, she thought, and kept thinking it. But the people did not look. She watched them walk away and wished they would turn around and take her with them. She wished they also didn't know where to go.

She was surrounded by steep hills of pine. The lower the light fell, the higher the hills seemed to rise over her head. At dusk they turned from hills to mountains, a sight that made her feel that her mouth was dry from the train. She was a girl with a fresh mouth, and to prove it spat on the ground once, then again, and kept spitting. She did not want to live in a painting. Not in these hill-mountains. She would wait for the next train and go back to the city. If her mother wouldn't have her, then she would go to a friend's house and live there. She would steal from the fridge and go in and out of a basement or bedroom window.

'Over here!' said a man she hadn't seen coming.

'Yes?'

'Are you Tomasin?'

'I am.'

'Let's go,' Keb told her, coming up to the gravel pool.

The first thing she noticed was that his clothes were too big for him. She wondered whose clothes he had on. She didn't know that winter on Prioleau made the men thin.

'Who are you?'

'The water taxi. I bring everyone to the island,' he answered. 'I'll bring you.'

'Where are we going now?'

He walked in answer.

'I need a drink of water,' she said. 'I'm desperate.'

'You can have that.'

Keb walked ahead of Tomasin down a dirt road. She didn't know dirt roads. He walked to the docks. She didn't know docks. She walked to the edge and looked at the water breaking below. The edge of a staircase, a bridge, or the edge of another person – these compelled her. Edges made Tomasin want to go over edges.

Keb picked up a tin cup from the bottom of the boat and held it out. She took it but didn't understand. 'There's nothing in this cup,' she said.

He took it back, reached off the dock and dipped it in the lake. 'Oh,' she said, taking it back. 'Is this your boat?'

'It is.'

He helped her in and untied the ropes.

'What do you do?' she asked.

'You work in the kitchen,' Keb answered.

'What?'

'That's what you do. You work in the kitchen.'

'Maybe I'm going to but I don't yet.'

She looked into the cup but couldn't drink. She couldn't drink because drinking water pulled from a lake was obviously a special and lovely thing to do, and she didn't feel like doing something special and lovely.

As the boat took off, the wind drew tears from her eyes. She expected so much but had no idea what to expect. She didn't try to hide her face from the man. She held her head high like a boxer, showing it off at a loose, tempting angle. Keb thought things might go badly for her.

Tomasin had always been lazy but was somehow fit, with small round shoulders and high hips. She had a long walk. She was strong enough to help the boys down at the docks before and after her kitchen work. They let her join them because she was new blood. Anything new that far out was embraced and would be known. Her face was not impressive but small and indistinct under a tangle of blond hair she never brushed. She had green eyes that didn't open very wide, and when she didn't get enough rest, which was most of the time, her eyes were red-rimmed. These red rims were threatening, but she was only sixteen and what could she do. They liked having her around. During her first couple days with them, she kicked a fishing rod into the water, ruining the reel, and broke the tip off another rod by jamming it in the corner of the boathouse door. She coiled ropes so badly they unfurled of their own accord like snakes with full stomachs. She cut the inside of her hand trying to sharpen a knife on the hand-crank whetstone, then showed off her bandaged hand at every chance. But she also swam way out without complaining about the cold. She was good and bad, they wouldn't overthink it.

Most of the boys were privately ready to give in to her purpose, whatever it was. Jer LaFleur was first among them. A young guide, he would put his hand in the mouth of a wolf to see how rough the tongue was. The head guides, Noah Coke and William, were men and married, but even they paid attention to Tomasin. She was entertaining, at least unpredictable. The Ware brothers, Sean and Adrian, wanted to know more. Only the youngest, Philip, was afraid, but he'd never had a girl for a friend.

Tomasin had her choice, she could feel it, and she chose the least likely boy to be hers. She chose him because he resisted. He never turned to look at her as she came down off the path to the dock. He had long hair like a girl, and it was the darkest hair she'd seen. She was jealous of his hair. He never came over and talked; the loudest racket he made was the rush of rope through his hands, while the others banged around in the hulls of their boats. He was always gone for the night before she could touch his arm to say goodbye.

Tomasin and Marie were on the porch in the early morning, waiting for Anuta to call them into the kitchen. Marie stood with her back against the wall of the lodge, looking out at the water. She was thinking about nothing, which she loved to do but could never make happen. To think of nothing was, in fact, one of Marie's favourite things to do.

Tomasin was making the blood rush to her head by folding herself over the railing. She liked the feeling of the pressure building behind her eyes.

'Who is that?' Tomasin asked Marie, swinging up and pointing to the low path.

'Who?' Marie answered, not looking.

'That!' Tomasin said, blood pouring down through her shoulders. 'Who is that boy, Marie?'

Marie saw Tristan walking to the docks. 'No,' she answered, shaking her head back and forth, 'not him.'

'No what?'

'He keeps to himself.'

'Why?'

'He does, that's all.'

'But who is he?'

'I don't know,' Marie said, lying. She pressed her back hard against the wall and hoped more or less to fall through it. 'I guess he's nobody.'

'Nobody?' said Tomasin. 'I like that.' She leaned over the railing again. 'I want to know him. He must be more than he seems, Marie. He's not nobody.'

'Leave him alone.'

'I feel like I know him,' Tomasin said, trying to tell the future. 'You don't know him.' Marie was the only one who did. Her father and mother knew too, but wished they didn't. Marie was the only one who wanted to know.

'What's his weakness? What do you think gets to him?'

'I don't know what you mean,' said Marie, pushing against the wall so hard it seemed to push back and almost pushed her forward onto her hands and knees.

Jer LaFleur wanted to know.

'It's late,' William told him.

'But what's with him? Say if you know,' said Jer.

It was late. The guides were on their bunks in the dark, within reach of each other.

Soon they would be in dreams and they were all waiting for that: to be alone. They were also vaguely waiting for Tristan to come home. He always came in late, after the lights went out.

He was an ongoing argument. He was present when spoken to but otherwise absent – if you wanted his attention, you had to say his name.

'He's always thinking,' said William.

'What?'

William was twice Jer's age, but Jer talked to him like they were young friends, urging him on. 'How can you tell?'

'By his eyes,' said William.

'His eyes? I haven't looked at them.'

'They're black-like.'

'Black like what?'

'I don't know.'

'This isn't helpful,' said Jer.

'Like night,' William offered. 'But not in here. Not night inside. They're like night out there, whatever kind of black that is.'

'I don't know,' said Jer. He didn't look at people's eyes. And besides, the night out there wasn't black. There were two huge moons: one in the sky and one on the water.

'If you don't know what's happening with him, that doesn't mean nothing's happening. It's like night. Lots happens, but you don't know.'

'He is like the night? Bullshit!'

'This isn't really about him, Jer. It's about you.'

'It is not.'

'You dig at him because you don't know what's going on in his head.'

'If anything,' said Jer.

'You can get anxious about everything you don't know, if you want. Like tonight, what walks past us, what flies over and how low? You don't know. If it rains, you don't know until you get to your boat in the morning and have to bail it out. You know less than you don't.'

'Oh yeah?'

'Yeah. I don't know either. But I know that.'

They fell quiet and listened to what the night was doing outside the cabin.

'Head like a cedar,' said Noah Coke calmly.

Noah was in the bunk below Jer LaFleur. He knocked on the piece of plywood that was the bottom of Jer's bed. 'His head is like a cedar tree, Jeremy! Do you get that?'

Jer laughed. Sometimes, as he floated off to sleep, he forgot he was in a bunk bed.

'You know how cedars look fresh and strong, but you cut into them and your saw falls through the middle? You have to watch your front leg.'

'I know that,' said Jer.

'There's nothing in there but damp air,' William added.

'There's a hollow,' said Noah Coke.

'Yes,' said Jer.

'That's what I'm talking about.'

'They grow like that close to the water,' said William. 'Hollow.'

'They do,' Jer agreed.

'Where do you go when you want to find that boy?' asked Noah. 'He's always at the water. The end.'

'Head like a cedar tree,' said Jer, laughing sleepily.

'Nothing in there,' whispered Noah.

Tristan had been dreaming but didn't want his dream and rose before the sun. He reached over the side of his bunk, picked up his boots and pulled them on, still lying on his back and bending his knees to his chest. By the light of thick stars, he walked the long way around the pitched and rocky northwest side of the island. He walked along the cliffs until they sunk into the water. Then he walked low, where the waves broke, stepping carefully from rock to rock, the water sulking below.

He sat on the rocks where he used to sit when he was alone. Of course his mother had been there, he had not been alone, but he did not want to think of her. If he looked out, he could imagine there was nothing at his back, no paths leading to stairs, no stairs leading to porches and doors, no walls and open windows, no tables planted with cut flowers, no strangers asleep in his house. He liked the beginning before the beginning of the sunrise, and this morning it lasted a long time. He didn't notice that he was cold until the sun slipped its fingers in between the treeline and sky to split a space open like the gills of a fish, showing the red breathing ribbons.

First light shed unsteady warmth like a young fire that was all kindling, thin sticks burning brightly and quickly. He reached his hands out to put them closer to the fire.

The sun soon woke the wind, which carried the kindling light wavering in all directions, in white and gold, until everything was lit. The fire wouldn't burn out but into daylight. Tristan pulled his hands back and rested them against his stomach. He was relieved it was over. The daylight brought warmth and shadows. The shadow of the porch over his head fell across his back and over the ground in bars of dark and light. One of the dark bars hit his sleeve and he shook it off like a spider.

'Hi,' said a voice dropping like another shadow.

He leapt to his feet, looked for the voice and tried again to shake the shadow off.

'Don't worry, it's me,' said a girl, climbing down the rocks behind him, and crawling into his hiding space under the verandah.

He shook his wrist to wick off a new shadow.

'It's me,' she said.

He didn't know her.

'I couldn't sleep. I don't know why sometimes I can sleep and sometimes I can't. It doesn't make any sense.'

He would have backed away, but his back was to the water and the rock sloped down like a sandbank.

Tomasin thought about introducing herself, then thought better: she would pretend they were close and soon they would be.

'What are we doing?' she asked, assuming he was out early for the same reason she was. 'I feel so restless,' she told him, sitting down where he'd just been. 'I guess we have to wait.'

He wasn't waiting for anything.

'I never watch the sunrise like this,' she said.

'The sun's already up.'

Tristan didn't know how to tell her to leave and never come back here.

It was funny, she thought, that he was pretending to ignore her when there was no one else. She looked at the side of his face, at his dark hair tucked behind his ear, then at his cheek, so soft it surprised her, like the cheek of a little boy.

Tristan leaned away under the pretence of picking up a few stones or a stick to snap into pieces, but nothing loose was within reach. He scratched a white line in black lichen with his fingernail.

Tomasin knew that sometimes you have to go through uncomfortable motions to make a friend. It could be like getting into tight jeans.

'Hey,' she said, calling to him even though he was close.

He turned.

'I've never seen that.'

'What?'

'You have the darkest eyes. And your lips too, they're dark.' In discovering them, she claimed them. 'I knew there would be something like that,' she said, smiling to herself and sitting back.

§

It was still early summer, a quiet day of no wind. On her two o'clock break, Tomasin went down to the docks feeling that all was possible, nothing necessary. 'I didn't come here looking for you,' she told Tristan affectionately.

'Okay,' he said, keeping his head down.

Bending over rows of fishing lures, he thought of covering them with his hands to hide them from her. He would have swept them up and held them against his chest, but the hooks.

'What is all this?'

'They throw lures away when the hooks are bent or stripped,' Tristan said, picking up a tear-shaped Red Devil. It fit in his palm. Two of its three hooks were gone. 'A fish will do this, or a snag. I take the bad hooks off.'

'Then what?'

'I replace them.'

'Then what?'

'That's it.'

Tristan's lures were laid out like patients across the warm dock planks. There were spoons and crankbaits in rows by colour: white and silver, silver with blue-striped backs, black with yellow bellies, and monotones in Crush orange and chartreuse. It made Tomasin remember her grasshopper hospital. She might have been six or seven when she set up the row of red bricks in the backyard. There were three holes per brick. She folded squares of toilet paper and tucked them into the holes for sickbeds. Then she scoured the backyard on her hands and knees for hours. She missed meals. She borrowed her mother's hairbrush to untangle the tall grass at the fence. But her desire to help the sick was frustrated, since all she could do was catch perfectly healthy grasshoppers that didn't need her help. Wiry, crisp-backed. They didn't need her until she pulled their legs off like she was plucking them out of the air.

Tristan clipped off the bent and rusty flaking hooks with small wirecutters that popped.

She enjoyed each pop.

'You don't want to scratch the paint off,' he told her.

Subdued by the sun and by him, Tomasin sat down. She looked at the eyes she'd discovered and liked them even more than before. They were darker than she remembered. But that was always their message: darker than you thought. His hair was almost the same length as hers, but hers was loose and white from the sun, while his was tied low at the back of his neck. It was purplish black, the kind of colour that rubs off on your hands. She wanted to untie his hair to see what it would look like down, and because she knew it would make him uncomfortable.

'How old are you?'

'If you don't line them up, they get tangled,' he said. 'That's why I do it in rows.'

She wondered if he was stupid.

'The new hooks will also break, or rust and crumble,' said Tomasin.

'I know that,' he answered, openly smiling.

'Just making sure,' she told him, then did nothing but smile back hard.

§

The verandah for Richter's parties hung off the edge of the island over water thirty feet deep. Tight and boundless as a pier, it inspired people to lean over its railing. It inspired commotion like a classroom, its sound carrying and breaking into echoes across the front bay, always slightly out of tune, since every night the piano was wheeled out into the weather's mercy, its wood painfully swollen midsummer. In winter, you could break a piece of the piano off like a square of chocolate, using your finger and thumb, but now the wood was so damp you could leave a thumbprint in it.

But if the songs were all sung out of tune, it was right – it would have been too much for the rest of the island if the music had been pitch perfect. Like this, it was faintly repulsive. It wasn't going to save any souls. It was no reason for the uninvited to feel bad about themselves.

Tomasin sat under the verandah because she loved parties. Tristan sat there because it was where he always sat. It seemed everyone above them had easy voices that split emotions like rounds of wood. They knew so many songs, when to quiet down and when to shout, when to snap their fingers. Tomasin rolled her shoulders and mouthed the words. Tristan crossed his arms and legs and looked at his crossed arms and legs, at his knees sore from working, now bent at a painful angle. He wished to stretch his legs out but was too self-conscious to move a lot.

He tried to look out, away from himself, but couldn't. The calm he usually felt when he came here alone was gone. If she didn't know the words to the song, why was she pretending? She sang a little behind the words, almost in round, her fingers flickering and picking at the air as if there were berries there. She couldn't be still. He thought about taking her hands and pinning them down. He took a look at her long, narrow legs and arms – not a lot of strength.

'If you can't dance, one thing follows the other,' she said.

'What?'

'If you can't dance, you can't be a good lover. I've heard that.'

Tristan tried to see the water, the two round islands to the east, but his eyes held an afterimage of her forehead and face, and her hands. The hands were bright as if lit. If this was how it was going to be, he needed to leave.

'I know what your weakness is,' she told him. Maybe she could feel how weak he was then, as the singing grew louder. People joined in and the piano followed their lead until the dance was almost frantic. They were not laying their burdens down up there, but throwing them. 'To hell with it!' a voice cried, and more voices knew to answer, 'To hell!'

Tristan wondered what it was, and why they wanted it to go to hell. Tomasin kept saying 'To hell!' under her breath like she was in on it.

'My weakness?'

'Oh yeah.'

'You have to tell me now.'

She didn't feel like it anymore.

'You have to tell me.'

'It's the way you are.'

She picked more berries out of the air.

There was nowhere for him to run. This was where he came when he ran away.

'What I'm saying is hard to say.' She was annoyed to stop dancing to answer him, feeling more akin to what was going on above, to all the people she didn't know.

'I don't understand,' he said.

'You're the same as everyone. But you think you're different.' Tomasin didn't believe anything she was saying and didn't know why she was saying it. 'You don't talk, you don't hang out, you hide under this porch.'

When he didn't answer, she looked to see how he was taking it. He looked so withdrawn into himself that she felt nervous and kept talking. 'But so what,' she said, 'to hell with it, you know. To hell, who cares!' Then she pushed him.

The further from his hiding spot he went, the weaker he felt, and now he felt weak tonight even before leaving. It felt like he was slipping down toward the water. He would roll a cigarette, he decided, but as he tried, his hands slipped and he spilt tobacco on his jeans. He only had a little bit of tobacco from Noah Coke, so he picked at his pants and at the ground to collect it.

Tomasin laughed at him, ready to push again.

He rolled the tobacco and bits of dirt into a cigarette, put it between his lips, and now – with smoke filling his mouth and going down – he could breathe. His breath spread out in front of them, reminding Tristan of the width of the calm that was only his, not hers. He would wait her out.

Marie didn't want to know. Tomasin was working the dining room at breakfast, and every time she came through the swinging door into the kitchen, she brushed across Marie's side or back.

'What a long night.'

Marie tried to step out of the way but was bumped again, this time at the hip. 'That hurt me,' she said.

'When I'm tired like this, it means I was really doing something, you know. I like being tired.'

The sky was encouraging her, Marie thought, looking out the back window filled with light like a swimming pool. The sky couldn't be more blue. It wasn't the blue of clothes or bedspreads, not the blue of a pen, and not even the blue of painted things, like the handles of her father's tools, which he painted blue so everyone knew they were his. Marie slowly grew infuriated that she could draw no comparison between this blue and something that she could put her hands on. It was infuriatingly blue. The idea of blue. Not her idea. It was someone else's idea, someone like Tomasin.

Marie called for rain.

Tomasin pushed herself on Marie, waist to waist. 'It's not going to rain,' she said, 'fuck that.'

Marie could smell her and liked it, but couldn't say what she smelled like.

Girls like Marie were supposed to defer. As if it would rain – there had never been a more blue day or a less urgent morning.

It was the kind of day things happen for people, or at least people like Tomasin. Not that there were more people like her. There were people like Marie, of course, but no one like this – if there had been, Tomasin would have been the first to admit it and to change herself.

Marie saw Tomasin's green eyes, red around the rims. 'What should I do?' she asked, pinned at the counter by Tomasin's hip and pelvic bone, one then the other.

'Nothing.'

'I'm sorry,' she offered.

'Sorry for what?' said Tomasin. 'You don't have to say sorry for being wrong. It's its own punishment.'

'I'm just sorry,' she said.

'Well, I hate it when people say sorry for no reason. Even if there is a reason, I hate it. What they want' – Tomasin pressed right in – 'is for you to feel sorry for them.'

'That's not what I want,' Marie said. She could only think that Tomasin was beautiful, but dreadfully.

'You should never say sorry,' Tomasin told her. And here was this tendency of hers to tell someone something that she was really telling herself: 'Whatever happens, just never say it, Marie.'

'Okay,' Marie answered. She was sweating around the neck. So was Tomasin, sweating and smelling of something Marie still couldn't name but liked. It was her skin.

Tomasin pulled off and Marie went to the sink to wash her hands. She had washed them earlier but it seemed like a lot had happened. She ran her hands under the cold water and held them there, spreading out her fingers. It wasn't right to ask the lake to do something for you. It was stupid. Rain for me, she had said, sorry to remember it. There was no rain on demand. It was the kind of thing Richter and his people were always saying. They thought the sun should shine when their skin ached for it; and later, when their eyes were tired, they thought clouds should roll in. Marie cupped water in her hands and rinsed her face, wiped the back of her neck and the front of her chest, then dried her hands against the sides of her dress, over her thighs. The modest dress she was wearing became less modest. Here was another embarrassment, but who would notice.

It was suppertime and they were out on the steps, the two Wares, Jer LaFleur, and Noah Chaperone, as Noah Coke liked to call himself when there was no one to talk to but these boys. Tristan was also there, but not with them. After work, he'd been so hungry that, as he knelt to rinse his hands off the dock, the water didn't feel like anything. He'd stirred his hands around, put his wrists in deep, but couldn't get to the cold. His hands were too hungry to think. Now he sat near but not with the others, not touching his supper, two sandwiches on wax paper across his knee.

Tomasin's arrival interrupted them all, but she went straight to Tristan. 'What now?' she asked, as if they'd been spending the day together and needed to choose the next thing. When he didn't answer, she talked about herself. 'I worked all day and can feel it in my legs. I said, Anuta, have mercy, let me sit down. I told her I can't take it. She said I don't do anything, why am I tired? I told her doing nothing is exhausting. I thought I couldn't take it, but I took it, you know. The bell rang. There is no bell but you know what I mean. I was so tired leaving, I fell down the porch stairs. Missed the top step. I might have liked falling, enjoyed it, but I'm not sure if it hurt. I think it hurts.' She was looking at Tristan now, at his mouth. She wanted him to say he knew what she was talking about. 'Right now, this second, I feel like I could run on the same legs that wanted to buckle all day. What is that?' she asked him. 'You aren't listening to me.'

He wasn't sure if he was listening. He stared at his sandwiches.

'I want to run. Do you feel like running against me?'

'Right now?'

'Now or ever.' It was so frustrating talking to him, and she liked it.

'I know how to run,' said Tristan, 'I could run.'

The others watched them, and their laughter and looks were like bits of shot, meaningless one by one, but together delivered a blow. Tristan stood up to leave, gathering his sandwiches.

'Where do you think you're going?'

'I don't know,' he said.

Where he was going, she would go.

Tristan didn't have conversations, so he didn't know how to get out of them. He didn't know conversations never end, they're only abandoned.

'Hello?' said Tomasin.

So overwhelming was his desire not to be seen anymore, or to be considered by her, or anyone, that he stopped breathing. His eyes, so dark no one could see in, turned dark to him from behind, until he couldn't see. He rubbed his eyes and stretched the skin around them.

'Hey,' Tomasin said, shaking his arm.

It was like being awake in bed in the middle of the night, eyes open, but there was no light to scrape things together. It was like those nights in the shed with the lamp and no oil, just the smell of it on his hands from digging in the bottle.

'Don't go anywhere,' Tomasin said. Something was wrong, she could tell – his body was so tight it was twisting.

He was thinking about how his mother used to tuck him in too tight and he couldn't move his legs. He would pretend to fall asleep, then wouldn't be able to sleep all night.

'What is it?'

'I'm so hungry. I haven't eaten all day,' he said.

'Come on,' she said. She would help him, but he had to come with her.

'No.'

'Come on.' She took his hand and tried to pull him, but he pulled his hand back.

When Tomasin was insulted, she would say, 'This is religious.'

'You're religious,' she told him.

Tristan wrapped up his sandwiches in the wax paper and walked away holding one in each hand. Tomasin went to her friends on the stairs and told them, 'Look at him. He's religious.' Religious meant she couldn't understand and it wasn't her fault. She liked to place emphasis on the word, and did, putting her foot on the second stair, stretching her leg out, and they watched her. There was no putting emphasis on boys who pulled their hands away.

The wind was incoherent and the sun shook in its bracket. There would be storms, he thought.

Anyone who didn't go to Treble Island or to town in a caravan of boats was swimming and drinking down by the water. Tristan never went to Treble Island now. He didn't want to go there, and besides Keb had told him not to, saying he might run into Codas, and Codas still wanted to get rid of him and send him south. What was south? None of them knew, but 'I think he'd pay for your ticket himself,' said Keb. That was Keb taking care of him.

Tomasin said she wanted to get off the island, was there anywhere they could go? She wasn't afraid of storms and he should take her.

Tristan wondered what she was doing as she dropped her shirt off her wrist and slipped out of her pants in two pulls. She seemed to wander to the water though it was right there. He couldn't see her, only the dropping off and slipping into the blue. When she dove, he was relieved she was gone.

Tristan hurried to get into the water before she rose, but she caught him. 'Dive!' she cried. 'Dive in!'

'But I'm in,' he said, almost there.

'You have to dive for the way it feels!'

Standing on the shore rocks, he watched her somersault in the shallows, her skin flashing black and white like a fish pulled up to the surface.

'I'm coming over there to get you,' she told him. 'Let's dive together.'

He would have to tell her he didn't dive now.

'Why are you standing there? Can't you swim?'

'I can swim.'

Tristan had brought her here, to Breaks Bay, a place of warm shallow coves, because he would only swim where he could see the bottom. He would never swim in deep water again after his mother was gone. Deep water made him feel like he was falling asleep. His feet stopped kicking a lot. His legs grew heavy to his waist. Where he could see the bottom, he could fall only that far.

'Let's dive. Tristan, please.'

'I don't have to.'

'No, you don't have to.'

'Thank you.'

'But you might.'

'I can't do it like you.'

'I'll teach you!' she said. 'I will be a wonderful teacher for you!' She would love to teach him something.

He kept standing there with his hands in the water.

Tomasin pulled herself out, first her small round shoulders, her bare stomach, all the way. And she dove again perfectly. She was showing off, he knew, but didn't blame her. He wanted her to be impressive, too.

She came in for the last time and started to dry off. 'Come on and get out,' she said. 'You're shaking.'

He was shaking.

'Come here.'

He let her tell him what to do. And when he reached his clothes, she was leaning over next to him, hanging her head and wicking her hair with her hands. They'd forgotten towels.

'Use your shirt,' she said.

She threw on what she always wore, jeans and a loose buttoned shirt. He watched her do the buttons and roll her sleeves. Sometimes she wore a shirt with the sleeves cut off but not today.

'Would you throw me my undershirt?' he said. It was on the other side. 'The white thing.'

'White?' she said, holding it up.

'White but you can see through it, I guess.'

Tomasin shook it a couple times to straighten it out. 'This?'

'That.'

It was a woman's shirt, Tomasin thought, almost a dishrag, but a woman's.

'Can I have it?'

The shirt made her affection for Tristan grow more serious somehow.

'Please,' he said.

She didn't throw it but handed it. She liked him more and more. Usually she liked people less and less.

On the way back to the island, Tomasin talked and Tristan listened. Dark clouds gathered in the north and bore down on them and made the water they were pulling their paddles through darken.

'If you don't know how to dive, what else don't you know?' Tomasin called back from the bow.

'I don't know if we're going to make it home right now,' he answered her, pressing his cheek against his shoulder to stop himself from smiling. He was so happy to be back out on the water just in time for the storm to come. It would make things hard for them, which he liked.

'What do you mean?' Tomasin asked, turning around to face him. 'If we aren't going to make it home, where will we be?'

'I don't know,' he said.

'Okay,' she answered, looking at him still. 'Just wondering. But I trust you.' And she smiled too.

What darkened was only Prioleau: the water dripping from their paddles, the waves, the near shore too thick with trees to land – these things, but not them. They moved through the new dark in danger but with little care, with only what they felt for each other then, and they felt light. They were radiant.

They couldn't see anything but water. It poured down their faces and arms and swished around their knees in the bottom of the canoe. There was no such thing as direction. When lightning lit up the sky, they saw only more water. Tristan cared for pulling through and nothing else, and he somehow knew that she cared only for what they were doing too, pulling without knowing where they'd come to land, ducking now and then in reflex to the strikes of lightning that felt close, even warm. They bowed their heads, couldn't see and didn't mind.

There was a small raised cabin behind the lodge where the workers went to break and for cards and drinks late. It was also where the three dock boys slept, Philip and the Ware brothers.

Sean and Adrian Ware were confident boys where they came from, but awkward here. They were from the city and used to places that were flat and well-lit, like playing fields. Philip, on the other hand, came from a farm about an hour and a half north of Prioleau. The land there was dirt over rock, a layer so thin it scraped off where you put your foot down. His family blunted their shovels and sharpened their shovels until their shovels were nubs. If you asked them why they farmed that land in particular, instead of land that had some give, they would say it was where they lived. Philip had come to here to make some money and would split it, one half for his parents and one half to buy an ATV.

The Ware brothers called Philip 'Baby' because he was smaller than they were, only fifteen to their sixteen and seventeen, with Sean the eldest and biggest by at least four inches around his waist. But there was nothing baby about Philip since he was all sinew. Not a strip of him would give under your finger – you'd feel only his pulse, like a pulse coming from a table where you've rested your elbow.

Along the right wall of the cabin, there was a bunk for the Wares, and along the back a cot for Philip, which wasn't bad and almost suited him, hard as a cot himself. They called their cabin 'the Crib' after dock cribs, those underwater rock piles packed into criss-crossed log walls. It was Noah Coke who came up with the name. He loved naming things and hated building dock cribs, standing in the water and wrestling with the logs so freshly peeled they bobbed, rolled, and slipped as he tried to drive foot-long nails into their thick middles. Then there were the rocks to fill the big basket. They had to be found on far shores, lifted and carted by boat to crib-side, where they had to be pulled again up your thigh, then pushed off your stomach and in. Noah always ended up swimming, either to fix a twisted log or to find a few last rocks because he hadn't brought enough in the boat, then with his head underwater he would think about how useless this all was. The winter ice would make the crib come undone, maybe not this year but next year, and these same rocks would spill across the bottom like a bowl of cereal and get sucked in by the silt, inhaled. It was amazing how the silt swallowed things whole.

Everyone packed into the Crib like it was a market basket. They edged and were edged, not only by each other but by boxed dry goods, body bags of flour and sugar, loose columns of linen, stacks of plastic chairs, baggy boat covers, rolled sails, water skis, coiled ropes, boxes and trays of screws and nails, odd cuts of wood, buckets of paint and stain, and paintbrushes soaking in jars of turpentine. There were things they knew how to use, and things they didn't know how to hold. It was easy to lose things in there, but also easy to find something you didn't know you wanted until you had your hands on it. West of the fishing docks, past the tennis court, there was a workshop and storage shed, but it was more convenient to keep things here in the Crib, so that's what they did. They kept everything for the kitchen, the boats, general maintenance, and even wood and pipe work.

The smell of the Crib was pleasant to the initiated. But to the uninitiated, nauseating. It was like being in a tent: if you wanted to be alone, you got up and left. If you were in, then you were all-in. They made up games, or Jer LaFleur and Noah Coke did, then taught their games to the others. Mercy was a favourite. It was a kind of quick boxing match that was always okay because it was over before you knew it. It was a favourite, but that didn't mean it was fun. The Mercy rules were simple: you had thirty seconds. The count was kept by a third party who was usually biased, but that was part of it. One foot on the line. No singing or dancing. No scratching. If you wanted out early, you cried *mercy*.

It started to be Mercy at the clearing every night. If you were there, it meant you were in. The clearing was where they burned brush and trash once a week in a bonfire. It was inland, a short walk to a wide circle cut twenty feet around so no branch or bit of thicket could spread the trash fire and burn the whole island down.

Tristan's first fight was against Philip because they were 'the babies,' Sean Ware said. Jer agreed and it was decided.

Philip went straight up and knocked Tristan to the ground by pushing both his shoulders at once. He almost punched him, but not quite. Tristan fell into the ashes, where he stayed as the count ran out.

Standing up, Tomasin grabbed him by the waist and pulled him aside.

'You're bleeding,' she told him, putting her arm around him, insisting they leave.

'What?'

'It's your throat.'

He felt it with his fingers. It wasn't much. A cut on the loose skin under his chin. It wasn't from Philip, he thought, but from something in the ashes, maybe glass.

'You'll do this, but you won't even dive?'

'I'd rather,' he said, nodding, making his throat bleed more.

She didn't understand that he had to do what they said. He couldn't say no. If they told him, 'Stand here,' he stood there.

'You left yourself wide open,' she said, taking his hand now since they were out of sight. She showed him how to press the cut to stop the bleeding. 'Hold it there,' she said, 'don't let go.'

He held it.

'Your hands were hanging at your hips.'

He didn't care that he'd been pushed down by Philip. He didn't care that his throat was cut. These weren't the kinds of things he cared about.

On Friday afternoons, the docks boys took the *Bellfly* to town. The *Bell* was for heavy supplies, what Keb couldn't carry in his boat: tanks of propane and gas, lumber and hardware. This Friday, on the deck of the *Bell*, the wind was all muscle. It pushed them around and pulled at their clothes. If the Wares had come north for adventure, here it was from all sides, above and below. Sean Ware thought of his car accident last year, feeling each wave hit the side of the boat like a car driven into them, a gross blow and a splash of lake water like glass.

They didn't know you couldn't get between the lake and land and just stand there. You couldn't cornerboy. There was no talking or hoping the water into their complacency. The boat sat low, held by its load, making it hard to turn. Sean the eldest held the steering wheel flush to one side, then the other, but the boat didn't answer. Waves blew over the bow and rushed to stern, rustling around their ankles like dead leaves.

The Wares weren't used to the weather affecting them. Philip was used to it, but on land not water. Richter watched them through his binoculars from the lodge verandah. He passed his binoculars to his friends, one by one, as the boat sat hunched in the storm, unpredictable, like a tied-up animal. Only it wasn't tied.

Richter's son Emiel took the binoculars. 'Should we do something?'

'I'm not in charge of the boats,' said Richter, looking for his drink and brushing the hair off his forehead.

'But you own the boats, they're yours,' said Emiel, watching the boys on the *Bell* run in soaked boots from bow to stern, then back to the bow. They were younger than he was.

'Maybe they'll knock the motor clean off the back of the boat and it'll sink to the bottom,' said Richter, sitting down and drinking. 'How many hours would they have to work to pay that off?'

'Two summers,' said Emiel, 'at least. I guess you'd own them.'

'Do you want to own them?' asked Stella, who'd just arrived on the island. She'd come reluctantly from the city to such a quiet place. She had also come in a water plane that had terrified her – 'a car with wings.' Richter had asked her to come to his island, then Emiel had asked separately, now she didn't know who to keep company. 'Maybe they'll throw themselves over-board,' she said, 'solving everything.'

'They're throwing ropes to shore,' said Emiel. 'But no one's there to catch them.'

'Let me see,' said Stella, coming close and taking the binoculars.

'Someone has to help them,' Emiel told his father. 'They're lost.'

'They're not lost. They're right there.' He brushed the hair off his forehead again.

'Richter, find someone to help them,' Stella agreed. 'They're throwing ropes to nobody.'

Richter put on his wind slicker and walked, because he never ran, to the guide cabin. At the door he knocked, but didn't wait for an answer, because it was his door. He lifted the latch and went in, and without hesitation announced, as if to a great crowd, though there were only four: 'The *Bell*'s floating off the deep swim. The boys are unmanned.'

The deep swim meant the cliffs west of the lodge. Noah Coke thought so what. Jer LaFleur thought it was funny. William had just started smoking a cigarette and was going to enjoy it. He wondered what the others were thinking and hoped one of them would do something, so that he wouldn't have to get up from his spot at the window. He had no plan to get up for a long time.

Richter did not want to see the crowded beds draped with towels, the patchwork bedding and beer-bottle ashtrays. He saw hands, and he saw arms wider than his, and a bare chest in there somewhere – Jer LaFleur's impressive bare chest – and more bare shoulders, and bare faces. It was easy to talk to the guides down at the docks, but this was something else. He could smell their wet clothes and sweat and the smoke from their cheap shag. It occurred to Richter that for the most part, these men, when they got to talking, probably agreed on things. But he had no idea what they talked about on a rainy night.

'Let's go,' he said.

Tristan knew how to get to the deep swim. He knew it better than anyone. That's what he was thinking as he volunteered, standing up and walking past Richter into the low light. He didn't stop for an extra shirt or coat, even though lying on his bunk under a blanket he'd been cold.

Someone was in the water. It was Philip, the farm boy. The idea had been for Philip to reach shore and then catch a rope, pull in and take hold of the boat. But Philip didn't swim to where he could climb out. He was holding on at the bottom of the cliff. Tristan watched him slide his hands across the wet rock and jam his fingers into crevices, then try to pull up, but the waves around his legs and waist were too strong and pulled him down. He had to push hard off the cliff as he fell to avoid scraping against it.

Tristan waved his arms to catch their attention.

'You see him?' Adrian asked his brother.

'I see him,' said Sean.

Tristan signed for them to move down shore and started going there himself. He led them to a narrow place where the cliff dropped in steps. There were a few small cedars growing on the last step. They could tie the bow to them.

'Not him,' said Sean.

'What do you mean?'

'I don't trust him, I won't follow him.'

'Why?'

'The way he is,' Sean said, holding the boat off. 'I don't like it. Let's wait for Philip.'

'Philip's useless, Sean.'

'He wants me to go in there?'

'He does.'

'If it's shallow, we're fucked.'

'He wouldn't wave you in if it was shallow.'

'I'm not doing it.'

'Please,' said Adrian. 'Please do it.'

'What, are you afraid?'

'Sort of.'

'You are.'

'Yes.'

They brought the bow in and threw the front rope to Tristan. It seemed thrown short but he caught it, and then all at once leapt to the bottom lip of the cliff and tied up to one of the cedars. The tree was too small and there was no time for a tight knot, but Tristan knew it would hold long enough. He looped the rope, dropped it, then jumped and half landed aboard. Using the light fixture on the nose of the bow as a handhold, he pulled himself onto the *Bell's* high front, hurrying because the wind was bringing the bow in to land. He ran to the steering, pulled Sean out of the way and took his place, shifting the *Bell* into a hard reverse for a second to knee-knock it. The motor roared and snapped its teeth at the water, pulling the heavy boat back. It worked: the bow kissed the island, not a passionate kiss but a chaste one.

The slack bow rope tied around the cedar now tightened, and for a moment the boat was still before the stern started to swing, pushed by the wind. Adrian cried out, 'Hey, it's Adrian!' wondering how they'd spent all summer within spitting distance but hadn't talked.

Sean could only think he'd been grabbed from the steering. Never in his life had he been handled like that by another boy, never mind one so effeminate and small.

'The wind's going to do you,' he said over Tristan's shoulder. The bow was tied, but the stern was swinging inland.

Tristan went to the bow, opened the crawl-space hatch, and pulled out the anchor. It weighed forty-five pounds but he lifted it easily, too easily for his size, they thought, watching him run to the tail of the boat, where he let the anchor drop. He was dispassionate about letting go. He didn't look down, only felt the rope run loose through his hand until it caught the bottom, giving him command of the *Bell*'s fat back end.

Tristan tied the anchor rope to the stern like a shoelace, looping and cinching it. All was right now, but something felt wrong as he stood up and straightened his neck. His hair was undone, falling across his eyes and down his neck. His hair tie was gone. He ran his hands through his hair, pulled it back, and would have tied it. When he let go, it fell back down.

'How do we get to shore?' Sean asked, stepping close to him. Since Tristan had grabbed him, Sean felt free to use his body too. If he could get this kid who moved like a little animal talking, he would be able to corner and still him.

'Leave him alone,' Adrian interrupted.

'Are we supposed to swim home?'

'No,' said Tristan.

Something about him was provoking: maybe his long hair, but that wasn't it. It wasn't just that he looked like a girl. A lot of boys could do that. He didn't say hello. He didn't even look at you.

If only Tristan's face had been one of those blank faces, they might have dismissed him, but his forehead expressed intuition, like he was listening to something at a distance they couldn't hear.

'You're landed,' he told them and, at that, walked the length of the boat, pulled himself onto the bow, and without pausing to measure the distance jumped.

Adrian hoped he would make it.

Sean hoped he'd go down.

Tristan jumped into a wall of trees, touching their bark with his boots and hands, but too lightly. Slipping into the water under the bow, he pulled himself up by grabbing low cedar branches in both hands. He pulled them clean off. As he reached for more, the bottom lip of the cliff came up against his knees and cracked them so hard his throat closed, but he never stopped moving. He reached for new branches, grabbed them just as hard, pulled, and ran a bit on his knees before standing.

Tristan cut across the main path. He didn't want paths. He wanted to open his hands and did and held them out, and as he walked and ran, he let them scrape across the rough bark of the pines. Draughts of cool air rising from the rain-soaked ground blew through his fingers. 'Her hands were torn,' he'd heard them say about Rachel, and ever since then he'd wanted to tear up his hands. Running away from her, Tristan used to come to the far side of the island and walk until he was too tired and hungry to keep going. He'd sit and wait to make her sorry. But what did she have to be sorry for? He couldn't remember now.

The night she didn't come home, he'd thought she was playing his game. At first he laughed about what he might say when she came back: 'You must be hungry. Would you like to share some of my supper?' But they didn't have any supper to share because she hadn't been there to make it. He might have said anything. But hours became a day, a day days, and the weather went through so many changes he couldn't remember them. There was fresh snow. The fresh snow hardened and more snow fell. He should have looked for her and never slept. He should have gone out with the lamp. There was so much oil then.

Mr. Matthews told him, 'You stupid boy. You should have told me.' But Tristan didn't know Mr. Matthews the night Rachel left. By the time he told them that he was alone, weeks had passed. Mrs. Matthews moved around her kitchen, went to the sink, pulled things into it, and washed them. They were already clean.

'You have to follow someone when you think of following,' said Mr. Matthews.

Tristan wondered if he'd done it to himself.

'You're not to blame, that's not what I'm saying. I'm just saying next time follow her.'

Tristan walked to his lookout on the far side of the island facing west, where the sunset would be most indelicate. But he was late, the sky had already bled into colours like dried flowers. There wouldn't be more sunset now, only a fading of light. He thought about watching it happen, but felt such unrest he couldn't stay. He looked across the mulled water and thought about climbing down and getting into it and going all the way out. But he would never do it. He didn't want the deep water and didn't care if it wanted him. He didn't even want to remember what it felt like. It was her lair now.

Marie and Anuta were leaving for the day when they crossed him on the eastern path. Anuta looked away because Tristan made her feel self-conscious. She didn't know why she should be. She told herself he seemed to be doing well.

Marie could tell he'd been out wandering and envied him. Why had she not been out wandering? She envied the one boy no one else would. So many things were possible for the two of them, and nothing happened. She had lost Tristan as her friend over and over. The worst part was how she made it all up and it was never a real loss.

The others were going to the clearing to play Mercy. And was he in? Jer LaFleur asked, coming up behind. Someone was already counting. It was Tomasin. If she couldn't fight, she would count. Tristan was in. He wanted to go where Tomasin was going. He would go with her and get her to leave with him. He would listen to her talk about anything.

When he saw Sean and Adrian, his breathing grew tight. Pouring concrete footings, he breathed in the dust of the dry mix and it felt like this. Sean was walking next to Tomasin and as they reached the clearing they stayed together.

Sean's pants fit tight to his thighs. He had persuasive shoulders and leaned way over with them to hear what Tomasin was saying. Tristan didn't like how Sean's hair was almost the same blond as hers.

'Hey.'

Tristan hadn't seen Adrian coming. He was another Sean, but not as tall.

'Tristan?'

They knew each other's names but had never said them to each other.

Tristan wanted to know what Tomasin was thinking. He wanted to know if Sean was comfortable in his tight clothes. No one knew what they were doing here, or what they wanted. He would admit it. He felt new things were possible, and some of them might be good, some were terrible.

'I don't know what I'm doing here,' said Adrian nervously. 'My father sent us. But he's the one who likes the water. I don't know what I'm doing,' he repeated. 'I guess you saw that.'

Tristan was half listening. He worried that Sean was talking as casually and intimately to Tomasin as Adrian was talking to him.

'I go to school. That's all I've ever done,' Adrian said, teasing himself. 'Not like you. Do you know what I mean?'

Tristan didn't know.

'I'm good at sports too, but not like Sean,' Adrian went on, hoping through these confessions to apologize for how they'd needed his help.

Tristan didn't know school or sports.

'Don't tell them I said this, all right,' said Adrian, meaning his brother, 'but I'm sorry for before.'

Sean turned to Tomasin and said, 'Promise you won't look.'

'Look at what?'

'Promise.'

'I guess I promise,' she said.

'Over there.'

She looked.

'I said don't look!'

'I didn't.'

'So, is he a boy or girl?'

'Tristan?' Sean knew Tristan was her friend.

'I want it to be me and him today.'

'No,' she said, but without moving her head from his.

Sean didn't think she meant it. He stepped into the loose half-circle that was forming and it closed around him.

Jer LaFleur said Sean could choose.

'Adrian!' Sean called out.

'What?'

'Just kidding.' He'd crush his little brother.

They all looked and laughed at Adrian because he'd lose.

'What about you?' he said, turning to Tristan.

'Who?' asked Jer. Jer wanted to be chosen.

'Him,' said Sean, but Tristan didn't answer.

'Only if he wants to.'

Tomasin wanted to stop Tristan from consenting but didn't try. Maybe she wanted the wrong thing. There were things about Tristan she didn't understand. Maybe she could learn something by watching this happen.

Adrian stepped into the circle and asked his brother, 'Are you kidding?'

'I was kidding about you,' Sean said. 'I'm not kidding about him.'

Tristan took two steps in.

'Don't,' Adrian told Tristan, holding out his hand. 'You're so small.'

'Adrian,' said Tristan, looking at the hand, 'it's okay.'

Adrian was so surprised to hear him speak – it was the first time Tristan had said his name – that he could only whisper back, 'You don't have to.'

'It doesn't bother me.'

No matter what happened, there would be this: they would step up, shaking out their arms to make them loose, and before the first lash, they would meet each other as matters of fact. He would be that, even taken down, even doubled down.

Tomasin started to count.

Tristan looked at her but she wouldn't return his look, not really, she would only count. He kept looking.

Sean stepped up and punched down, thrusting his fist into Tristan's mouth.

Only after he was hit Tristan did lift his hands, but not to fight or protect himself. He lifted his hands to feel the wet. He was still standing somehow. No one said anything, only listened to the count. No one thought it odd that Tomasin kept counting; silently, they counted too. Only after Tristan broke the circle and was a few steps away did they start calling his name and telling him to come back because he had to try harder than that. He had to try, they said.

Jer LaFleur told Tomasin to go get Tristan, knowing she could. He knew she was close to him, they all did.

But what did they know? If they knew so much, could they explain it to her?

'Go talk to him,' said Jer.

'What do you want me to say?'

'Say something.'

'I'll tell him something, let me think. Hey! Come back! They want to fuck up your face.'

Tristan was holding his bottom lip in his mouth, sucking on it and hiding it from her.

'Let me see it. Let it go.'

He wouldn't.

'You're religious,' she said, 'let me see.'

He let go and his lips parted. His top lip was whole. His bottom lip was split like a bait worm into two loose pieces.

'Christ,' she said, only whispering, as if talking might make the cut worse. 'You need stitches.' But that didn't matter to him. What mattered was her mouth, familiar to him. It was small. If one of them had a perfect mouth, that was good enough – it didn't have to be his mouth.

'You have to put your hands up, Tristan.'

He had to?

'Do you hear me?' she said, still whispering. 'You have to.'

He sucked on his bottom lip, half smiling at her. 'A ring on his finger,' he tried to say, fumbling his lip. 'He's wearing a ring.'

'He doesn't wear rings.'

'He put on a washer.'

If she wanted to touch Tristan, she had to pretend to do it by accident. But they could hit him across the face with washers on their knuckles. They could not only touch but crush him. She'd been thinking of trying to kiss him, but now his lips were in pieces and wouldn't heal for a long time.

'They're yelling for you,' she said. 'You didn't say mercy yet.'

She would have liked to feel what it was like.

He nodded and sucked on his lip.

She walked him back. It didn't occur to her that she might do anything else.

Tristan and Sean stepped into the circle.

'Nervous?' said Sean.

Tristan looked over at Tomasin, maybe to say go ahead, start the count, or maybe something else.

Sean wanted Tristan to look at him.

Tristan was still looking at Tomasin when he was hit in the high stomach. He kept looking at her. Now he knew what he wanted to say. He wanted to ask her, 'What was that?' He hadn't seen Sean coming. It was as if she'd hit him.

Two punches landed: the first in his stomach, the second against the side of his head.

'Surprise,' Sean said.

Tristan dropped to the ground concussed. And the Mercy circle fell apart like a beaded necklace. The string snapped and the beads slid off. Tomasin watched the others run. They weren't accomplices to Sean, but must have felt more than just themselves. It wasn't enough to split, they had to keep splitting, running

not only away from Tristan – face down, he'd fallen on his face –
but from each other too. They ran alone: Sean, Adrian, Philip,
Jer, Noah Coke. And Tomasin was left holding the string of the
necklace in her hand, kneeling over Tristan. His body had
bounced, she was sure. He wasn't bouncing anymore.

Noah Coke came back down the path. He'd been running when
he remembered these were children. It was a children's game.

The boy was on his stomach. 'Let's turn him,' he said.

She turned the shoulders while Noah turned the legs.

Not only Tristan's lip, but his nose was bleeding. His nose
was bent flat against his cheek.

'Is he asleep?' she said.

'I don't think it's sleep.'

Tomasin rubbed Tristan's chest to comfort him and herself.
She wiped the blood from under his nose and dabbed it off his
lips with the back of her hand. But she couldn't clean the blood,
only spread it around.

'When will he wake up?' she asked. She liked touching him
like this.

'I don't know. I never know when he wakes up,' said Noah.
He didn't know the boy. Nobody did. 'The rest of us wake up
together, you know. He gets up and goes before first light. I think
he's done for the night now.'

Tomasin leaned over Tristan to shade his face, though there
was no point, it was getting dark. She wished Noah would go.
She laid claim, put her mouth to Tristan's ear to whisper something. But she couldn't think of what to say and just left her
mouth there.

Noah wondered if Tomasin knew him. She had no experience
knowing people, he could tell. But children did have ways of
understanding each other.

Tomasin tried pushing Tristan's broken nose back into place,
but couldn't, or she could but it wouldn't stay. She tried lifting

him. 'Don't help me,' she told Noah, wanting to do it herself. She tried carrying Tristan in her arms. She tried getting him on her back, but his body was all relaxed. It wouldn't cling or attach.

In the morning, William and Noah Coke talked to him and rocked him. They all tried, even Jer LaFleur, but they couldn't wake him up for work. The sun rose, the light filled the air over the water, came to land, and cut the island's paths open, but Tristan wasn't there. He was asleep with his hands clenched. Jer LaFleur tried to pry his fingers open, but it was no good.

He slept through sunrise, all morning, into the late afternoon. When he woke finally, the cabin was stifling, the air thick with the heat of midday and the feverish heat of his body. He was covered in blankets up to his chin. William had pulled them up in the cold of early morning, but now the air itself was as heavy and prickly as an old blanket. Tristan pushed the blankets off, but couldn't push the air.

He woke again, this time with a terrible pressure in his face. He tried breathing to ease it, but breathing carefully only made the pain worse. He leaned over the side of the bed and dry-heaved, leaned more and threw up, then fell back and kept falling until he was asleep.

'I can't believe you,' she said, 'you should see yourself.'

It was Tomasin.

'I've been here. When I couldn't get away, I sent Marie. You know Marie,' she told him. 'Marie is Marie, she's useless. Though not completely useless. She can run an errand. But generally, she is. Why am I talking about her?'

He tried licking his lips, but they were swollen and pungent and disgusted him.

'Of course you woke up for me,' she said, sitting at the side of the bed, putting her arm across him. 'I brought you an orange juice. I'll bring you other things.'

The thought of juice made Tristan feel like throwing up again.

'I came in here and she was holding your hand, or at least she had her hand near yours, right here on the sheet. I'm talking about Marie,' said Tomasin, showing him, taking his hand. 'She had her hand here.'

He didn't like to think of people touching him in his sleep.

'I wasn't going to tell you, but I guess I couldn't help it.'

He didn't like to think of people touching him when he was awake either, and she had his hand. He didn't need to take it back – it could be left out flat – but he needed her to let go.

In his sleep, she'd touched his ear with her mouth, his forehead and hair, and had thought about kissing him and would have if his lips hadn't been ruined. She was young enough that her sex didn't have any blood in it. No, she wouldn't touch blood: it was too much the other person.

Nothing was his, not his hand. If he had ever wanted to believe he owned anything, Tomasin was the end of the illusion. She held the glass to his lips. It wasn't orange juice she'd brought, but orange crystals half-dissolved, and she'd made it strong – stronger than anyone else would. It stung the tear in his lip and coated his tongue. It was grisly mixed with dried blood, but he sipped because he was thirsty. And because if he didn't sip, she would still tip the glass.

'I have to go, but drink the rest of this,' she said, putting the drink down on the floor below his bed. 'And by the way, your nose is broken, so don't touch it. It has to set, you know, like a cake.' She was leaving. 'You want it to have some shape.'

From under his bunk he pulled out Rachel's mirror – like an old letter, but sharp around the edges. Holding it made him feel better. He knew how to hold it on a slight angle to catch the light from his window to show his nose and the top of his mouth. Cotton pink with blood was stuffed up both nostrils and he pulled it out, only to have his nose sink into his cheek. He tried putting the cotton back in, rolling it up tight and handling himself roughly. His nose took some shape back but stayed bent. He'd never seen anything like it: he had to try to recognize himself.

They met under the verandah at sunset and there was new respect, or new disrespect. She wanted something from him; he was disappointing her somehow. She didn't like that anyone could be so unaffected by what she wanted.

'Why did you do it?' she asked. He'd let Sean hit him.

'I don't know.'

'I would understand if you were good at it.'

'You know I have to fight around.'

'I know that?'

'So they'll leave me alone.'

'You are alone. They don't come to you, you go to them.'

Tristan thought he'd never gone anywhere. This was his home. They had all come to him, even her.

'I have an idea for you. You don't look good,' she said.

'The swelling is bad,' he agreed.

'It's not the swelling.'

'I don't care what I look like.'

'I care.'

'It's not useful to care,' he said.

'If you take a spoon, you could use it, you know,' Tomasin said, reaching out to touch his face, 'to fix this,' but he flinched and pulled back so she missed him.

But Tomasin kept reaching and took a loose piece of his hair instead. 'There,' she said, tucking it over his ear, 'much better.'

He was thinking you can't fix faces with spoons. He was also thinking he could still taste blood.

In junior high school, Tomasin and her girlfriends had tried to change their faces using anything they could get their hands on: creams from their mothers' cupboards, sand from the edge of the driveway mixed with the creams to make an exfoliating paste. They made plasters of flour, water, and strips of newspaper: papier-mâché casts. They took naps wearing the casts. They talked on the phone wearing them, and tried to sleep in them too, but the masks would fall off in the night and crumple under their pillows. After this, they'd made splints for sleep, which involved tying scarves around their heads to hold glue and popsicle-stick frames. These were never any good, but it was worth a try. And they did the spoon thing, massaging for hours in front of the TV, working the bottom of the spoon in hard-pressed circles, breaking the soft shells of cartilage cells, bruising the tissue to make it malleable.

With the sun gone, the piano took its place as what they were doing. They didn't hear it as the sun set, now it was all they heard. It sounded like a toy piano against the silence of the water and far islands. Tristan imagined he could pick up the piano in one hand and crush it like a pop can, or if he couldn't crush it, at least throw it into the lake. But if he did that, it would be a fixture, the water's currents forever crossing its keys and strings, and once in a while a note would strike, and more notes on that note's back. And what would that mean?

'I wonder what this place was like before, you know? Before the piano,' said Tomasin.

He knew the piano was heavy, but it had wheels. He could roll it to the Mercy circle and light it on fire.

'Do you wonder what it was like?'

'No,' he said. If he told her everything, she wouldn't understand.

Never, until Tomasin, did Tristan tell any part of his story. And to her, he wasn't telling it properly.

'Well, I wonder.'

It didn't feel good to be with her, not exactly, but he was starting to like how it felt. It didn't have to feel good. She didn't need to be better than she was, or to know what she was talking about.

§

It was Sunday again, and they pushed out into open water toward more open water. Tomasin didn't have to ask, he would take her somewhere she'd never been. There was so much sun that the water, low at their sides, was a harsh white, like snow shelled in ice. The waves were white and gold, and the water pouring off their paddles made pocket-size rainbows. If they looked straight down, the sun seemed to shine up from the bottom of the lake three hundred feet below.

They closed their eyes and flicked them open, not needing to see everything, only the notch in the neck of the distant shore that marked their passage.

Tomasin hoped the notch was a narrows that would take them from here to somewhere forbidding.

Tristan never hoped for anything out on the water.

'Looks like sand,' she said, leaning far over the side.

Tristan leaned hard the other way to save them from tipping.

They were in a shallow cove. The water was only three or four feet deep and clear to the bottom. The bottom was white but ribbed.

'I want to walk on it,' she said, wanting to drag her feet across the ribs.

'There are beaches in all these coves. No one knows they're here.'

'But you.'

'I guess.'

'You know everything,' said Tomasin.

'I don't.'

'Yes, you do. Don't argue,' she said, turning to look at him. 'Let me enjoy it.' She would have moved closer and made him close his eyes so she could press the lids with her fingers – she wanted to cover his eyes then uncover them – but she was stuck kneeling in the bow, so instead she laughed. They weren't supposed to know anything, but they knew some things. These were their beaches.

The sun flooded the water and reflected off the sand, and here and there it reflected off the bronze sides of smallmouth bass. Their black backs and white-tipped tails flicked in chase of clouds of finger-length minnows.

'What is that?'

He told her they were minnows.

They moved in schools. She'd never seen them. One school shot under the canoe, came up and pooled alongside it, then circled toward shore.

'They can swim anywhere,' he said, 'in an inch of water.'

'I can't think and watch them at the same time,' she answered, trying to follow them. 'It makes me nervous.'

'I can,' Tristan said.

The minnows slid through the water like slivers. Tristan knew to rock back and give them space, or they'd break away. They followed nothing but each other. They crowded – they cinched – coming so close they could only push off each other. It was intimate, but too much, so it was estranging. The cloud slowed and split into a hard rain of light. When the minnows lost each other, they lost themselves, casting out like a knit mirror. Tristan wondered what they would do without the smallmouths to chase them. Would they split up? They might sliver into nothing, dissolve like salt.

'Come on, it's shallow enough for you,' Tomasin said, slipping over the side of the canoe in her shorts. The water reached her stomach.

'But I'm tired,' he said.

'Tired?'

'From the sun.'

'Come in with me. It'll make you feel better. The cold water will be good for your face too. Like ice. You're still swollen.'

'I know.' He still couldn't breathe out of his nose. 'I'm coming.'

'No, you're not. You're just sitting there.' She wanted him to feel what she was feeling, the cold water around her waist.

Tristan almost felt ready to begin. He might say, 'Do you know why I don't swim anymore?' He imagined Tomasin might say, 'Tell me everything.' He wanted to tell her how Rachel disappeared in winter. Little boys, younger than he was, seven and eight years old, found her in a place like this, a cove, in the water. After breakup, after the thaw. They were wading in and flipping rocks to catch crayfish. They came back with a bucket full of their catch. They'd found her. They knew what she was. They'd found her but had wanted to fill their bucket until the rim was crawling. They must have lost some crayfish on the walk back.

'I don't swim where I can't see the bottom,' he said. But that was all he could think to start.

'I know that,' Tomasin said.

'I don't do it.'

'I already know that. It's shallow here,' she said, walking away from the boat, pushing the water with her thighs in a way she liked. Was he watching this? She felt commanding, even to herself, making it hard to understand how he could resist her. All she wanted was for him to come in.

She pulled fistfuls of sand from the bottom and covered her arms and the back of her neck. She shaped it to her skin, and it relieved the tops of her shoulders, which were so burnt they glistened even before she hit the water. She held still until the sand dried enough to crack and peel, then bent her knees, fell back in the water and went under for a long time. She washed it off only to pull more from the bottom. She liked how it was as heavy as a hand and pressed against her. It made her want to be touched, so much that she went to Tristan and rubbed sand on the back of his hand. She shouldn't have to ask him to touch her.

'Do you know what you are?' she asked, putting more sand on the back of his hand and rubbing it in.

'What?'

'Mine.'

He watched her cup water and pour it over his wrist and hand to rinse the sand off. It was a relief, what she'd said, and a disappointment. He'd briefly hoped she would tell him that she knew everything already, so he didn't have to tell her. She only washed his hand.

'I decided a long time ago. I'm just telling you now,' she said.

He wanted to tell her everything, and he would, if she would ask the right questions.

She wanted him to be only this.

Tristan felt like lying down in the bottom of the canoe. He thought of the girl Marie who'd sat in Keb's boat all those days. He'd watched her, waiting for her to try something.

'Come in the water,' Tomasin said, telling him now. 'Come, Tristan,' she said.

He slipped into the water and brushed off the last bits of sand she'd put on him, and for hours they waded in the shallows and filled the bottom of the canoe with rocks and driftwood. Tomasin saw faces in the wood and told him to look. She saw the wings of birds and the more elaborate wings of angels. 'Bird or angel?' He told her, 'Whatever you want.'

They pulled the canoe up and stretched out on the rocks beside it to dry off in the wind and sun. Tomasin peeled out of her jean shorts, wrung them dry, and hung them over the side of the canoe.

'You should take off your wet clothes,' she said.

He didn't want to. They were already drying.

'I wish we had something to eat or drink.'

'Drink from the lake.'

'I always forget that.'

They laughed and stayed outstretched, their hands cupped over their eyes for shade.

'I can't sit up,' said Tomasin. 'Now that I'm down, I'm down. I can't even raise my hands.'

Tristan agreed, and they laughed more because their bodies felt not their own but sunk into the rock.

'If you weren't here, I might have died of thirst. We should always be together,' Tomasin said, 'or something bad might happen.'

Tomasin didn't know what she was doing with him, if he wasn't going to give in. He knew what he was doing, what he always did.

She was at shore getting a drink, cupping her hands, when she felt him touch her shoulder.

'Hey,' she said, dropping the water and turning to knock his hand.

'Hey,' he said, bringing his hand back to her shoulder.

He was putting something on her arm, the same way she'd put the sand on his hand. But when she tried to brush it off, it stuck, a thick, claret black, and Tomasin thought it was dried blood.

'What are you doing?' she cried at him, spitting on her hand and rubbing her arm, but she couldn't rub it off, only in.

'It's okay.' He wanted to explain. It was something his mother had put on his shoulders for sunburns. He would tell her.

'It won't come off,' she said, disgusted.

'It will come off.'

'Tell me what it is.'

'Why are you angry?'

'I'll hit you,' she told him.

'Don't.'

'I've seen people do it to you.'

He was trying to tell her.

'What is it with you?'

If she wanted to hit him – if it would make her feel better – then he would let her do it. His face was already hit. It didn't make any difference.

She'd been waiting for him to touch her and now this. 'Tell me,' she said, pointing at her shoulder, holding her arm as if she were holding a fresh injury.

He wanted to tell her. His mother had put it on him as a child. She'd rubbed it into his shoulders.

'You like it,' she said. Tomasin stood and jerked, threatening to follow through: 'I'll hit you.'

'Don't,' he said.

But he didn't care and she could tell, stepping through herself and swinging. She hit him in the side of the forehead, a small packed blow.

'Oh!' he cried, taking his head in his hands in a crouch. The rocks were ragged and sloped toward the water. He didn't want to fall down there.

'Why did you cry out?' Tomasin shouted at him. 'Why did you just cry out?' She was disgusted with herself and with him. She'd never heard him cry out the other times. She worried about what it meant, readying herself to hit him again, should it be necessary.

Tristan didn't try to defend himself, only told her, 'This isn't good for you.' It wasn't good for her.

'What are you talking about?'

'Do you feel better now?'

'No, I don't,' she said. 'But it's not for me. I hit you for you.'

On the right side of his forehead, just above the eye, bluish lines pushed through the skin like veins from exercise. When she swam as hard as she could, the veins in her forearms bulged like this, but around these lines there was a red and then a white rim. They were marks from her finger bones in tricolour, and Tomasin thought of her favourite popsicle, the Rocket, with the same colour scheme. She would never be able to eat that popsicle again without thinking of this.

His eyes were tearful. So were hers, but she didn't know. Why was everything up to her? Why was he crouching over like that? Why didn't he stand or fall? One or the other. She wanted to hit him again, at least one more time.

She went into the water because there was nowhere else to go.

Tristan eventually sat down and held his head and fingered the bumps she'd given him. He couldn't think, only feel the bumps. He mapped them to her fingers.

They stayed that way for what seemed like a long time, ignoring each other and thinking only of each other.

It was a tin for peppermints. He twisted the lid and it was full up to the rim with a black cream. Using two fingers, he peeled some out and spread it across the back of his hand and rubbed it in. 'It's sunblock,' he said.

Tomasin hated the way he was concentrating. She wanted him to concentrate on what mattered.

'Who showed you this?'

'No one.' He wanted to tell her.

'What is it?'

'Poplar tree,' he said. 'It's rotten. It gets soft like this and you can dig it out. It makes sunscreen.' When his mother remembered, she would put it on his shoulders. She only remembered sometimes. Other times, his shoulders peeled until the skin was mottled bright pink and white.

'I can't believe you touched me with that shit.'

It was painful to be on that shore, so immense and at peace with itself, and to be so small and so at war. The air was full around their faces and necks, but a strange breathlessness overtook them. The branches over their heads swayed and the brush behind them shook in the wind, but they couldn't easily breathe.

'I don't know what's wrong with you,' she spat out.

'I don't know,' he said.

'You could act like a normal person.'

'I would.' He didn't want her to be unhappy with him.

'There's what you want me to think about you and there's what I think, and they're not the same, Tristan,' she told him.

He didn't want her to think anything. He wanted her to stop shouting at him. When she shouted, she ruined her mouth. She put her body in her talk. Her bare legs tightened against him.

He put his head in his hands to hide his face. 'I don't feel well,' he said.

'You're religious, do you know that? You do something to me, then you want the pity.'

They were in the Crib, rocking in chairs that weren't rocking chairs, balancing on the back legs, taking pleasure in feeling the legs bend.

'You can want a lot,' Tomasin said, the back of her head pressed against the wall for balance.

'Like what?' asked Jer LaFleur, joining her by rocking back and pressing his head against the wall too.

'Hi, Jer.'

'What are you talking about now?' he asked. She was always talking.

'You can't want what he wants.'

'Who?' Jer couldn't talk in riddles and balance. She needed to be specific or he needed to sit down. 'Do you mean Tristan?'

'He tried something.'

'Tried for you?'

'He reached out and touched me. I wasn't even looking.'

'He got his hands on you! Is that what you mean?'

'He didn't even say anything,' said Tomasin. 'Not my name.'

'Don't be too hard on him,' Jer said, bringing his chair back to ground. As tough as he was, he didn't like being hard on people.

'He didn't get away with it. I hit him in the head.'

'In the head?'

'Right in the face.'

'So, what are you worried about? Sounds like you took care of it.'

'I think it's what he wanted. He wanted me to hit him,' said Tomasin.

'Why?' asked Sean, who'd been watching them.

'He lets you beat him in the face because he doesn't like how he looks,' she told Sean, still balancing.

Jer was ready to catch her. He thought she would fall.

'You help him,' Tomasin told Sean.

'I do not,' he said.

'He doesn't like his own face, that's what I think.'

'I don't help him, Tomasin. I don't do anything.'

She rocked forward and reached her hands across the table toward Sean. She wasn't offering her hands but showing them.

'You're right,' she said, 'you don't help him. But only because it won't work. If it could work, then you would be helping.'

'What are you on about?' asked Noah Coke, interrupting her to make her stop. To him, Tristan was a little boy, and a boy like that couldn't do anything wrong that mattered.

'He has this stuff,' she said, pulling her shirt down at the neck to show them her shoulder. 'It's cream. What boy puts on creams?' She showed them a burgundy circle on her shoulder. 'Do you see? That's where he touched me.'

The boys started to laugh because they didn't know what else to do with her. Noah Coke wasn't laughing. He knew that Tristan had put sunscreen on her.

'It's not funny,' she said.

She kept her shirt off her shoulder.

'I don't know,' Adrian whispered to his brother.

'You don't know what?' Sean whispered back.

'She's not right about everything. Not like she thinks she is.'

'I don't care if she's right,' said Sean, 'and I don't think she cares either.'

§

She always came, but if she wasn't coming, then he couldn't wait and would visit the docks and bail the boats. He usually bailed to feel the earliest sun – the docks faced due east – and to be close to the water before anyone else was awake, to smell the oil and gas and ropes. Sometimes he bailed out every boat, then the others came down and no one knew it had rained in the night.

Today he bailed because Tomasin had not come to see him last night or this morning. He had waited for her. He lunged with the bailer, scraping the bottom of the boat, spilling half the water back. He didn't know what he'd done wrong, so he didn't know how to work it off. He knew it wasn't by bailing these boats.

'What do you need?' Anuta asked, stopping him at the door.

'Hello,' he said.

'Hello? You have to wash your hands before you come in here.'

He left and came back holding out his washed hands.

'So what do you need?'

He didn't need anything. He tried to get inside, but she blocked the door. 'You still can't come in. We're working. I don't know why I told you to go wash your hands. It doesn't make any difference.'

There was something desperate in names, thought Marie. She didn't want to yell his name after him. 'Hey!' she shouted, 'Hey!' Her love for Tristan stood in front of her like another person she had to shout over and climb around. She would climb overtop. She would claw. She would somehow put love down, though she wasn't confident she could: she had never done it. After all, love was unwieldy – when she reached out, it grabbed back, grabbed her wrist, and twisted until her fingers went numb, love did.

If love stood between her and the world – if it interfered with her knowing anyone – if this was how it always was, maybe this was who she was. This was her, running after him down the path, unable to say his name. He didn't turn. 'Please!' she tried. She would give him the letter she'd written. It was tucked in the bottom of her tackle box under the weights. She didn't have any good lures, so no one would ever sort through them and find her letter, she was safe.

She ran but tried to make it look like she wasn't running. She ran every few steps.

Tristan heard her coming close. 'Have you seen Tomasin?' he turned to ask.

'Tomasin?'

'She was supposed to meet me,' he said, looking into the near trees like he might find her there.

'Tomasin?' asked Marie, trying to understand, looking where he was looking.

'She's missing.'

'Tomasin is sick with a fever. But Mum says she's not sick. Maybe she is. I can never tell with her.'

It was time for Marie to go back, but she looked across Tristan's face a few times. She couldn't look straight at him and take it all in. His eyes were a sore black. There was a cracked scab down the middle of his bottom lip. What she cared for above all – his eyes that were almost his mother's – had little to do with her own life. How could that be right?

'I'm going,' Tristan said, not knowing kindness to recognize it.

'All right.'

'I'm going,' he said again, because she kept looking at him like she didn't understand.

'Why did you run away? Why did you do that?' asked Anuta.

'I didn't run,' Marie answered her mother. She had tried not to run. She had run every few steps.

'Be better than that.'

'No, I can't,' Marie said.

'You can't what?'

'I can't help it.'

'You can't help opening the door and throwing yourself down the stairs after him?' said Anuta. 'You can.'

'I can't.'

It was something Marie had always suspected but never wanted to admit. She couldn't be anything. She was what she was, crying through closed eyes. She couldn't make her eyes listen. She couldn't make her heart listen and stop its pounding below her throat. Her heart was what it was, in damp darkness. She put her hand over it. Why keep knocking at her chest when she was coming to answer? She was always coming as fast as she could. But the knocking was behind a wall, and there was no handle, no latch, no little hole to stick her finger in. She could only dig the tips of her fingers into her ribs.

'Well,' said Anuta, worried now, not by the tears, but how Marie was grabbing at her own ribs.

'Leave me alone.'

'I could have let you just come back in. But I have to tell you when I don't like something, Marie, when I don't think it's good. I have to tell you when I don't like someone.'

Marie convulsed at being told not to do what she would do again. 'There's nothing wrong with him,' she said.

'There's nothing right with him either.'

'I don't like that idea.'

'Go wash your face, Marie, and wash your hands.'

She went to the sink.

'Not the sink. Go to the wash basin.'

Tristan went to Tomasin's cabin. He found her on her feet. If one can wander in a small room with little furniture and only a few things, that's what she was doing: wandering around her room. And she was doing it in perfect health.

'Sick?' he asked through the screen door.

'Yes,' she answered, trying not to smile, though she didn't try very hard. She couldn't believe how easy it had been. She had prepared herself to wait days for him.

The island had its depths where people could get lost. It had cloaking cedars. It had pines so high and tangled with sky they blocked out the sun. The pines cast shade in patches like cool rooms set deep in a house. The more light of day, the darker and cooler these backrooms were. When she came down from her cabin, tucked high over the shoulder of the lodge, Stella could be imagined instead to be coming from one of these rooms, out of nowhere you'd been, at least not with her. She came out of nowhere. She was someone's daughter still, though maybe also a mother. Where were they now, her children? She was an actress, but played only once or twice a year because she did not like the parts for women in plays and films. On stage or an island, on a porch in the morning, stirring her coffee with her finger, just like this, Stella was of interest. More subduing than a migraine, she somehow became what you were doing. If she didn't acknowledge you, it felt personal. Emiel was annoyed with her and the day had just begun. The way she stirred with her finger and kept stirring long after the sugar was dissolved – this was personal. It all was, he thought.

When Emiel wasn't in the city he had a headache. What he would have given this morning to walk in a shouldering crowd, to be held up by the press of bodies and voices, and carried he did not care where. He had never understood vacations. He didn't know what to do with himself here. He didn't know what to think about. 'This place is desperately calm,' he said to Stella. He had never wanted to come, but his father made him. 'What am I supposed to do here? Am I supposed to meditate, Stella? Are you meditating?'

'I am not.'

'I have a headache.'

'You always have a headache.'

'I'm not asking for your sympathy.'

'You want to have a headache,' she said.

'I do not. Why would I want that?'

'For something to do.'

'No.'

'You're always doing it to yourself,' she said. 'We all are. It makes us great: we think about something a certain way and it exists. If we don't, it doesn't.'

'Like what?'

'Like your headache.'

'And what else?'

'Everything is like that.'

Stella was on her way to the docks when she saw the girl that interested her. She liked this girl because she had long legs and didn't know what to do with them. She wasn't an athlete, but held a strong posture coming from her hips, set high and pitched forward. Her hip bones stuck out above her jeans like a boy who wakes up and does two hundred sit-ups each morning. She might have been graceful if she were not so obviously restless. There was an unhappiness about her, vague, but it could be used. If this was Stella's prodigal daughter, where had she been? It didn't really matter. She was here now.

'Hello again,' she said, though there'd been no first hello. 'Do they hurt?'

'Does what hurt?'

'Your cheeks,' said Stella, 'of course they do.'

Tomasin's cheeks didn't hurt.

'They looked better before. But how would you know? Well, they were pale, only days ago, and the paleness made you look clear.'

Tomasin had never seen this woman.

Stella put her hand over the girl's right cheek and ear. 'I can't see through the burn. It's like you're blushing,' she said.

Tomasin passed the test by letting her face rest in Stella's hand.

'I know your cheeks are burnt and that you're not blushing, but that's what it looks like. I keep asking myself if you're blushing from pleasure. Is it because of me she blushes? Am I embarrassing you? I don't want to.'

Tomasin didn't understand what she was talking about and didn't care. She'd never met anyone so at ease with themselves. Tomasin loved her loose white dress cinched with a black belt. She could only think that somehow she'd been chosen. Usually, she did the choosing.

'And what's your name?'

'Tomasin.'

'It is,' Stella said in confirmation, as if she'd just taught the girl her name.

What use could she be? Stella wondered, holding the awning of her hat against the sun. It was her favourite hat, straw with a tight weave. It was a gift from an Englishman who'd come to the same play she was in for many weeks. He always sat near the front and stared at her with an anguished look on his bare face. Stella remembered seeing him implore his wife to give up her hat so he could make a sudden gift of it. His wife had put her hand on top of her head, right on top of the hat, and leaned away from him. But again he asked her. Stella read his lips: 'Please, she's not another woman, she's an actress.'

§

'I'll see you later, like before,' Tomasin said.

She'd almost crossed him on the wide path to the lodge, but he stood in front of her holding a stringer of lake trout, their speckled sides and black tails still wet.

'Where?' he asked.

'I always know where you are,' she told him, looking at his fish.

'I'm here now.'

'You have your hands full.'

He swung and gently laid the fish down on the pine-needle path, freeing his hands. Tomasin wouldn't come later. She didn't come anymore.

'I heard what you did,' he said to make her stay. 'Yesterday,' he said.

'Tell me what I did.'

One of the fish flicked its tail and made them jump.

'That's just its nerves,' Tristan said.

'Just its nerves? What does that mean?'

Now the fish lay quiet.

'I'm talking about yesterday,' he told her.

'Why do you need to know everything I do?'

Her eyes, as usual, looked sore, like she'd slept too long or needed to sleep now. If they were green eyes, they were green like water: black when you're swimming through it, but clear poured over your hand. There was nothing in her eyes to reassure him. If there was anything there, it was languor.

'I don't know what you're accusing me of,' said Tomasin calmly, looking back at him. It was all easier for her than it was for him, and it had something to do with what she was made of.

'You went out in a boat with people.'

'I did.'

He was the one who took her out on the water. He had over-heard the boys saying she'd gone out with a woman, and that Keb had taken them to Cross Inlet, and the woman had given her drinks out of a flask etched with a skull wearing a flower crown, and she'd been drunk and had smoked a cigarette so thin no one knew the brand. No one had seen a cigarette that thin. It was so special Tomasin had wanted to put it in her pocket, to show the boys later. The woman made her smoke it right there, put it in her mouth and lit it. Tomasin didn't smoke, but she smoked past the silver and light blue bands of the filter, tore across them like long-distance ribbons.

'I was with Stella,' she said, which meant nothing to him but sounded bad.

Tristan had never been to Cross Inlet. He had heard the shore was made of white quartz. He didn't think he should have to ask her, she should tell him.

'Do you know what she said? She said she liked my face better before. She doesn't like my face as much now.'

'Who said that?'

'Stella. Is it bad?'

'Your face? You're sunburnt.'

'I never see myself here. There are no mirrors, have you noticed that?'

'Why do you care what she says?'

'I don't decide if I care what someone says. It's not a decision I make. I care or I don't.'

'She doesn't care what you say to her, I bet.'

'How do you know?'

'Because they don't care what we say. I'm a guide,' said Tristan. 'You're not even a guide, you work in the kitchen.'

'You're religious. You're more religious than ever today.'

'What does that mean?'

'I'm going out with her again. You can't come with us.'

'I don't want to come. I wouldn't go.'

'No?'

'I don't want to.'

'You're jealous.'

'I am not,' he said, picking up his fish to go. They felt heavier than before.

'Maybe you see your hands. You can see the front of your jeans and shirt. You see that, fine. But you don't know what you look like to me. I see your face. I see what you're doing. You can't not be seen by me.'

Tristan turned his face.

Tomasin saw him trying to take himself back from her.

'I keep seeing,' she said. 'I'm leaving now and I'll still see.'

'Where are you going?'

'Don't ask me that.'

He would take her somewhere, if she would come with him.

'I'm going,' she said.

He felt like kicking her legs out. He wanted her to stay. He would agree to everything. He would defend her against herself. There were people here who would take advantage of her and she would let them do it. She would help them.

'You don't come around anymore. You just do what you want,' he said after her.

'You don't think I should do what I want?'

'That's not it,' he said, walking quickly to stay close. He could still trip her.

'Then what are you saying?'

Tristan put his free hand on one of her hips and pulled it back. 'You know who you remind me of?' he said.

'I hate that,' she answered, finally turning.

'What?'

'Comparing people. I'm not like anyone.'

She was probably right.

'I hate that idea. Never do that to me.'

'I won't,' he agreed. He would agree to everything, she should know that.

'Okay, now you have to tell me. Who am I like?'

There were so many things he needed to tell her. 'You're not like anyone.'

'Tell me or I won't talk to you again.'

'My mother,' he said. There was no feeling in him.

'What?'

'I don't know what I'm saying,' he said.

'This is stupid.' He was making her feel stupid. 'Your mother?'

'You made me say it.'

'Do you know why I don't come around anymore? Maybe it's because you make me feel like this. Tristan, I feel sick.' He loves me, she thought. How can I be free of him then? She couldn't let him do it anymore. She didn't ask herself how to be free if she loved him.

'You make me feel guilty and I haven't done anything wrong,' she said.

'You haven't done anything, I never said you did.'

'Do you know what I'm saying these days?'

'What?'

'I'm saying fuck you, basically.'

'What else?'

'I'm not saying the rest to you. The rest is for other people.'

He felt close to a fire where the air is eaten up. He wanted to get closer, to gather the locks of flame, coals, and blackened spit below. He would pick up the smoke and carry it.

It had been August for others, now it was August for him. The ghost flower was his harbinger, growing in the hollows of the pine roots on the back of the island. They stood shin-high, stalks of bare white holding out against the dark tide of the forest floor. There could be no better surprise. It was only for him. No one else came here, and the ghost flower was the strangest plant or animal on Prioleau's shore. Only long, round-bellied trout pulled from deep down rivalled them in otherworldliness. Root tip to flower, they looked lit from within. He picked one and tore it in half to see if it was white inside: it was. It made him remember something he didn't know, that he couldn't know, because he'd never asked Rachel. 'What happened to you?' he might have said. 'Did something happen?' There had been months on end he'd thought of asking but never did. He somehow knew his mother would never tell him. Then more time passed and he didn't see it anymore – the scar pitched under her eye like a tent over rough ground – and maybe that meant he didn't see her anymore. The skin under her eye was the same living white as this flower. It was a gift she'd given him: to know that not everything needed to be understood. Not every story wanted to be told. It was crude to remember everything. His stories didn't want anything. What's this flower for? he wondered, thinking nothing would dare to eat it, and nothing ever did; it just rose and fell like a weird wind. All it did was remind him of her. What did she look like now? He couldn't remember her face, and even if he could, what for? As if a face was for something.

§

Tomasin swore off Tristan dispassionately. That's how she remembered it, standing at the counter between Anuta and Marie.

'Have you come to work?' Anuta asked her.

'What else would I come here for?'

Marie had thought about Tomasin the night before while undressing. As she took off her clothes, they not only lost shape, as usual, but seemed to deteriorate. Tomasin was always in a state of undress. How she looked – was that how she felt? Standing over her crumpled clothes, Marie had felt akin to Tomasin. But if this feeling of wanting to throw everything away was anything like Tomasin's general feeling, it didn't feel good.

'Do you know what *hubris* means?' Anuta asked Tomasin.

Tomasin put her hands on the counter in surrender. 'No,' she said, 'sounds bad.'

Marie wanted to whisper the answer. Why did she have to be the witness? She looked at the kitchen floor and saw dirt and flour – the half-cup of flour Tomasin had just spilled, maybe on purpose. It looked like dirty snow and would be satisfying to sweep up.

'It means pride,' said Anuta.

Tomasin's hands flat on the counter were her answer.

Tomasin was a girl like a gang of boys. But wasn't she as harmless as Marie? Anuta had a growing confidence in Tomasin's defiance, since it thrummed like a boat crossing the bay – the more staunch the waves, the more steadily it banged on. She was the same every day and would be. What Anuta disliked was a woman who changed. She thought Tomasin would never change.

'I'm going to set the tables,' said Anuta, picking up a heavy basket of linens for the dining room. 'You two do your work.'

Tomasin looked at her hands resting on the counter and had to admire them. A girl didn't have hands like this for nothing. Her body was shy of maturing, she knew, but her hands were ahead, her fingers long and narrow. How come Tristan had never noticed them? He would regret it. She would show him her hands.

'Your forehead,' said Marie, looking at her hard.

'What?'

'It's tight and your eyes are red. You'll give yourself a headache. Can I help you?'

'Why would I need your help?'

'I don't know.'

Tomasin was supposed to cut a lot of fruit, but it was hard to care. She never cut her own. She just bit into it and turned the fruit over. If it was hard to eat, that was the best – to bring her teeth down on a pocket of seeds or a pit, to spit that out and feel the juice on her wrist. With her forefinger and thumb, she picked up a cherry and put it in her mouth, then closed her eyes and tongued the pit out.

'Placebo,' she said, spitting the pit onto the counter.

'Are you okay?'

'All better, Marie,' she answered, opening her eyes languidly. 'I haven't needed your help all my life. I don't need it suddenly.'

As Marie moved in to halve and pit the whole bowl of cherries, Tomasin pushed back, took a few more and ate them, spitting the pits out onto the counter like dice, as if their arrangement might tell her fortune.

The cherries came from down south and were expensive, Marie knew. They were too suggestive, her mother had told her. Marie often smelled them, dark and sour, on her fingers, but she'd never put one in her mouth. Because they weren't allowed to eat the cherries. As Tomasin spat another pit out, Marie imagined turning on her heel, reaching out, and nicking Tomasin in the side of the neck with the paring knife. The blade would cut as it touched. She provokes me, thought Marie, testing and rolling on her heel. That's all she would have to tell people, 'She provoked me,' and they would agree.

Looking at the stain under her fingernails, Marie suddenly felt guilty, as if she'd gone ahead and swiped the knife. She imagined putting her hand on Tomasin's neck and pressing the wound.

'What are you thinking?' Tomasin asked. 'You should work instead of daydreaming, Marie. You love to work.'

Let her eat the cherries, thought Marie. She cannot help it.

'Hello?' said Tomasin.

'I'm sorry, I'm here.'

'There you go again.'

'What?'

'You're always sorry.'

'I am?'

'Yes.'

Tomasin put her hands back on the counter and looked at them.

Marie tried it too, put her hands out. But she didn't like them. Every time she cut cherries the stain washed off, but that never stopped her from wondering if this time it wouldn't.

That night, Tristan sat under the verandah and rolled cigarettes. He would smoke them one by one and leave after smoking the tenth. If Tomasin didn't come by ten cigarettes, she wasn't coming. But she would come. She didn't mean a lot of what she said.

The night across his forehead felt like a cool washcloth. Tomasin had held a washcloth to his face after Sean broke his nose, and it felt like this, he remembered.

He didn't end up smoking the last ones but let them burn in his hand. The tenth he held close to his ear and listened while the thin rolling paper ashed like dragonfly wings rolled between his fingers. Dragonflies were easy to catch these days because the nights were cold and it made them slow on the dock in the morning. Their wings crumpled even when he was trying to be gentle. They flaked along the seams like late autumn leaves. It would be autumn. Soon she would go back home. He would still be here.

The dance floor above his head was more subdued than usual. The dancers stepped as if manoeuvring around a pool of water with soft sides, afraid to slide in. Did they see their reflections and not want to disturb them? He fell asleep sitting up, like an old man.

Her eyes were closed but she could still see the sun. Some of us are part god, Stella was thinking. It's my eyes or eyelids. Maybe the skin across my forehead. She put her hand there and it felt cool.

'What do you think?' she turned to ask Emiel, who was sitting in the chair beside her, reading his book. She'd abandoned Richter for his son to survive her vacation.

'About what?'

'What do you think of me, Emiel?'

'I don't like that question.' He did not look up. 'Not this afternoon.'

'It's a perfect afternoon.'

'There's a lot of sun. There's sun all over these pages. I can barely see.'

'Well, you don't have to see me. What do you think of me, I said. It's not complicated.'

'You always ask me the same thing.'

'I forget what you say.'

'You don't listen. You only want to ask the question.'

Emiel tried to be clear with Stella. If he left anything ambiguous, some little phrase or feeling, she would take it up, take off and be gone, dragging him behind her into the orchard of her imagination where strange things grew and stranger things decayed. If she handed him something to taste, Emiel knew to carry it for a little while, then put it down at first chance, but not so soon she'd notice.

'Maybe you're right,' she agreed, 'maybe I don't listen to you. If you started talking now, it's possible I'd ignore it.'

'Fear, Stella,' said Emiel. He wasn't reading anymore.

'What?'

'I don't think about you so much as fear you. I go from there.'

'Oh.'

'It's not good or bad. It's how I've always felt. In general, I fear you. I also fear you in particular.'

'What else?'

'I like it. I think I must like it, or I wouldn't be sitting here. I only want to sit with you.'

Stella sighed, almost satisfied.

'Why are you sighing like that?'

'I just felt sorry for you suddenly,' she said.

'Don't feel sorry for me. You never have.'

Stella would have said something more, but they were interrupted by Tomasin standing at the foot of their chairs. She was serving tea and coffee. And she was also doing something else, Stella thought. The girl was coming to her.

But she didn't want the girl right now. 'Come back later,' she told her. 'Come back later, but go now.'

Emiel was surprised. As Tomasin turned, she blushed all the way down her arms and held her own hands. 'Is she something to you? Do you know her?'

'Who?'

'It's nothing,' he said, understanding Stella wanted to keep the girl to herself. She didn't like sharing, and sharing people was her least favourite.

'She's new.'

'That's obvious. She's kind of awkward, don't you think?' he asked.

'What's obvious? She isn't awkward.'

'No, not really,' said Emiel. 'Just a little.'

'She isn't awkward. I think she's unhappy. It's different.'

'Yes.'

'I got her drunk the other day. She didn't know what was happening to her.'

'You would do that.'

'I did.'

'I'm not surprised.'

'Yes, you are surprised.'

Emiel didn't have to have his way with Stella. It was somehow enough that he understood her, that's what he told himself.

Tomasin didn't stay away as long as she should have, returning with two glasses of ice water, though they already had water at their table.

'Tomasin, you give the impression that we don't know each other. Come here,' Stella said, making the girl come down to kiss her on both cheeks. 'That's better.'

Stella's embrace wasn't easy to understand. It reassured, it threatened.

Tomasin wanted to put the water glasses down. With her hands full, she couldn't relax and hold herself how she wanted to for these people.

'I'm sorry,' she said, forgetting that sorry was something she never said.

'For what?'

'Standing here like this, with these glasses.'

'Forgiven.'

'Thank you.'

'You are forgiven because we are not in the practice of condemning beautiful women, are we, Emiel?'

'No,' he said, 'we don't do that.'

'We like them no matter what they do. Now go away.'

'Me?'

'I'm not saying go away forever, but for now, I'm with Emiel. I'm always with one person. Maybe this afternoon we'll do something.'

Emiel noticed that Stella was trying hard with this girl. She was holding her head at the most pleasing angles, checking them off a subconscious list with little ticks. She didn't have to show off her profile. She might have slumped and all would be well. Her neck – so long and thin but ribbed with muscle –

was a woman's neck but strong as any man's. Stronger than his. He ran his hand up the back of his neck into his hair. Only sculptors and surgeons were intimate with the kinds of detail Stella's body suggested.

'Go,' she said.

And Tomasin was gone. She went to the kitchen and looked around for the sink and couldn't find it.

As Marie took the glasses of water from her hands, still full, they tipped and spilled cold water over their wrists.

'You're sweating,' said Marie, holding back from wiping the sweat away.

'I am?' She couldn't explain. More was possible now. But more wasn't possible for Marie.

Marie put the glasses down and went ahead. She brushed her hand over Tomasin's forehead, then put her hand behind her neck and wicked the sweat. Then she pulled on Tomasin's shirt at the front to let in some air.

Tomasin followed Marie's hand across her face, and all she could do after that was take Marie's shoulders in her hands, pull her in roughly, and kiss.

It was a hard kiss. Marie's lips gave in and her mouth opened. She had not been kissed in her life. She couldn't tell if she had kissed back or resisted.

The song they were singing over Tristan's head felt like one endless refrain, a chorus over and over again. There was no restraint. It was night again and he was waiting for Tomasin. He tried to feel the right feeling, confident or indifferent, but neither came to him. He could feel only the wind between his shirt and skin. The wind was coming from the west on the night shift. It was making the bats eat early. He listened to the snap of their slick wings. He tried but couldn't see them, only hear their glide and flit as they came close to his face then whipped away, down over the water. There might have been one or one hundred – their black bodies and eyes had the same gloss as the sky, so there was no counting.

The wind was supposed to curl up for the night in a cove. But not this wind. He could hear it coming over the water and land, and he could see it in waves rising, their full backs reflecting the moon and stars until the lake looked like a crumpled map. His mother always said that a night wind from the west was an omen. He'd believed her once, but not tonight. The wind wasn't talking to him. If it was, he wasn't going to talk back. He didn't want omens.

'We'll wake to a change,' his mother would say. 'That's what a west wind means by rising as we're falling asleep.'

'What should we do?'

'Nothing different.'

When he woke the next day, nothing seemed changed. 'It didn't happen,' he said, leaning to tell her. 'Something happened but it was for me,' she answered, laughing gently. It seemed to hurt her to laugh, even gently, like laughter was coughing. She rose a bit and gathered him in her arms, and she held him so tightly that he believed her, and would believe anything if she would let him go.

Hungry and sick from chain-smoking, Tristan couldn't decide if it was a good idea to keep waiting. He knew how to be alone. He was good at it, he would tell her. It was something Tomasin would never be good at, and he wanted to tell her that too.

'When you get lost, don't trust your instincts.' He could do that. 'Stay where you are, don't go.' He couldn't tell if his mother had told him this, or if he was making it up. 'Wait for me,' she'd told him, or had she? 'I'll meet you there.' And then what? He looked to where he used to sit, when the island was his. Tight in his hand, he felt a stone he'd picked up without noticing. One stone at a time, he was throwing the island into the lake, and it was no consolation but it was true he was doing it. The island was disappearing, imperceptibly to everyone but him. It was hard to say what he missed about Tomasin. He missed the way she talked when she didn't have anything to say. He missed the way she felt so much when there was no reason to tell for her feelings. Every time she left him, maybe that was what he missed. When she walked away after a long time together, it was like the end of sunset, when less impressive, more suggestive colours take hold.

The lake was locked in peace under a low blue sky. As calm as it could be, she could see to the bottom twenty feet. The weather never matched her feelings. Marie could feel the clutch of her heart, clutch and release, with the letting-go like something falling off a table, calling only for another catch, another clutch. Her heart grabbed at the blood. She thanked god for the small bird stirring in the shore bushes below. It picked up and took off. The first snap of its wings and then she saw it, maybe a thrush. Maybe it was a thrush, but Marie didn't know the names of birds. She didn't want to know.

When a small bird took wing over the water like this, it was often to its death. The talons of the falcons that caught them were so sharp they couldn't touch, only cut. Marie searched the sky with a feeling of purpose – as if she could do something against the onslaught – and when no great bird screamed out of pines, she felt as though she had done it. Her will was a shield. The thrush was saved.

Marie had no grand illusion, but one small one: if something didn't have anything to do with anyone else, she could interfere. She could help a thrush because no one would know. And if they did know, they wouldn't care. As for the talons, the heat of them, the melt, they could sink in somewhere else. Into the next thrush – this one was hers.

Marie stood at the rail of the verandah doing nothing.

'Why don't you say something to me?' Stella asked her. She was alone.

'I'm here to bring you sugar,' Marie answered. The sugar was on the rail in a small cup.

'What are you waiting for? Bring it here. And while you're doing it, you can tell me something.'

'It's not eight o'clock yet,' answered Marie. 'Nothing's happened.'

'Where's the other girl, your friend?'

'She comes late.'

'Of course she does,' said Stella. The most restless girls were also the most lazy. She loved that.

'And I don't have a friend,' Marie added. 'Tomasin isn't my friend.' She said this, not for Stella, but to herself to be clear.

'Not a friend in the world?'

Marie lost sight of her little bird and was looking for it. 'If I don't have a friend here, then I don't have a friend anywhere,' she said.

'You might.'

'That's not fair.'

'Not fair?'

'If I have a friend somewhere else, it doesn't matter. I live here.'

'The shore over there keeps going.'

'The mainland?'

'Yeah, the meat. This is the scrapings.'

'I wouldn't know what this is, or isn't.'

'Have you had your eyes looked at?'

'No.'

'That explains it. You can see me?'

'Yes.'

'But you don't have vision.'

Marie couldn't find her thrush.

Stella wanted to brush her teeth. This girl made her feel like she needed to brush her teeth. 'May I have the sugar now?'

Marie thought about flipping it onto the porch. But that was something Tomasin would do.

'I know a lamb when I see one. If I'm wrong and you're a wolf, come back to me. Think about it. I don't really have to ask. If you're a wolf, you'll come,' said Stella. 'That would be so exciting if you were. It would make me wrong,' she said. Stella loved to summon and banish.

Marie went away thinking she wasn't a wolf or lamb. She could only wish to be something that easy to name.

It was the kind of morning they couldn't tell if it was mist rising over the water or clouds come down. Anuta and Marie drove their small steel boat slowly. The fog pressed against their faces like a beauty mask.

'We'll start up the generator,' said Anuta.

On a morning of fog or storm, they would start the generator to light the paths. This early, Anuta and Marie were sometimes happy to be together. They weren't awake enough to feel the need to define themselves. They couldn't think that abstractly, only feel the laced air. Their arms felt light – or Marie's did – buoyed by the fog and silence, and she assumed her mother's did too. Then the boat scraped against the dock, creaking like the opening of a huge door. Their footsteps knocked. When she was happy like this, Marie always wondered what sorrows of misunderstanding awaited her in the next hours, and could she bear them.

They found something wrapped in a dishcloth at the kitchen door. It was on the top step, pinned down on one corner by an empty jar.

'What is this?' said Anuta, stepping over it. She didn't want to know what it was. Something between the children.

Marie held back and, once her mother was inside, bent down and lifted the jar and picked up the cloth. It weighed less than she thought. A sugar cube or two, with most of the weight in the rag. She squeezed it and tried to guess. There was no note attached.

Marie knew it was for Tomasin. She would never have imagined that it was put together and left for her.

Tomasin was late.

'Your hair isn't tidy,' Anuta told her.

'I didn't have the strength to brush it, forgive me.' She liked asking Anuta for forgiveness to annoy her.

'Look at Marie's hair.'

'What about it?' She had no interest in Marie's hair.

The girls were appalled at being compared, even just their hair. And besides, it was crude: Marie's hair was dark and she wore it tied back low against her neck, while Tomasin's was flush-blond, almost white, and broke around her head like a beach wave.

'You could tie your hair back,' said Anuta, who hadn't thought it necessary before today, and wasn't sure why she was saying it now.

'Someone left something for you,' Marie interrupted them. 'I have it.' She went to her coat behind the door and pulled out the rolled cloth. It was so light she worried there might be nothing inside. 'It was at the door this morning.'

'How do you know it's for me?'

'It's not for us,' said Marie.

'Okay.'

'Are you going to open it?'

'Not now.'

'You should.'

'Marie, don't be naive. When somebody gives you something and they don't write your name on it, and they don't write their name down, you have to wait and think.' Tomasin squeezed the cloth at one end, then the other, and squeezed it in the middle. 'There's something in here,' she said. 'I can feel it.'

'What is it?'

'It's mine,' said Tomasin. Sharing something with Marie would diminish it.

Marie should have pretended not to care what was in the cloth, but she had never been good at pretending. 'I know it's yours,' she said. 'I just gave it to you.' Maybe she would start guessing when to pretend not to care. She might do it now and then at random. She didn't need to get it right. She needed to know what it felt like.

Confident that Marie wasn't watching anymore, Tomasin unwound the cloth. Out of the last turn fell a small warm thing. A ruby-throated hummingbird, sleek and dead. She screamed.

It's perfect, thought Marie, looking at its round chest that seemed mighty, no thicker than a thumb. The heart in there somewhere was hard to imagine. The size of a blueberry. You could pop it between your fingers. The feet were curled like a spider's legs when it fakes dead. She wanted to touch the feet to see if they were hard or could still flex.

'This is disgusting,' said Tomasin, dropping it and stepping back to the counter.

Marie reached out and tried to catch it on the way down. But she wasn't famous for her coordination. What little she had seemed to deteriorate when she felt desperate, as now. Mid-air, with unwieldy stiff fingers, she brushed the bird, causing a single wing to spread open and stick.

'Oh, sick!' cried Tomasin.

The bird hit the floor with the softest sound, more shocking than any crush or thud, as if the floor wasn't wood but grass.

Without hesitation, with her thumb and index finger, Marie pinched behind the tail and picked it up. She wanted to hold the bird against her breast, but it was much too small to embrace. She tried to close the open wing, but couldn't; to close it, it would have to break.

'Marie, please,' said Anuta. 'Put it away and wash your hands. Both of you, wash your hands.'

Marie wrapped the hummingbird back in the cloth and put it in her coat pocket. She would return it to Tristan and try to explain.

They all knew it was Tristan. Who else could catch a hummingbird?

Tomasin didn't understand. Did he mean to please her? Make her suffer? He knew that she loved watching the hummingbirds feed at the plants with the loose pockets, the foxglove on the front of the island. Would a fox paw slip into a foxglove? Yes it would, she had said, and he had agreed on it.

'There are things, you know, that people don't know about Tristan,' Tomasin said to Marie, whispering so Anuta wouldn't hear her. 'People deserve to know some things about some people.'

'There are things people don't know about you,' answered Marie, but then she wished she hadn't said it, and so to appease she added, 'There are things people don't know about me.'

'Like what?'

'Things, I guess.'

'When people know about me, I won't be exposed, Marie. But revealed. There's a difference. Does he think I want a dead bird?'

'He must not think that.'

'Then why wrap it up? Why make me unwrap it?'

'I don't know,' said Marie, 'maybe he doesn't think of it as a dead bird but something else.'

'No more of this,' said Anuta, coming between them. Turning to Marie, she ordered, 'No more talking to this creature.'

Tomasin leaned to whisper, not in Marie's ear but against the side of her mouth, 'What are you if I'm a creature?'

Marie didn't think she was anything.

'I'm getting on the train one day to come here, not to work. I'm going to sleep in late, drink your coffee, and eat your fresh bread. I'll put cinnamon and sugar on the bread after butter, then I'll eat only half, sit out there, read, and do nothing. You'll have to throw the other half away.'

'You don't read.'

'I will,' said Tomasin.

'I've never seen you reading.'

'So you're always watching me? Do you like to watch me?'

'You don't drink coffee either.'

'I'm talking about the future.'

Marie never talked about the future.

'You're talking again,' said Anuta.

'We are,' answered Tomasin in new confidence. Her confidence had a habit of suddenly renewing for no reason.

'Do you know the word *precocious*?' asked Anuta.

'I don't want to know your words.'

'You don't know it?'

'If I do, I don't care.'

'It's one thing to be precocious when you're brilliant. It's another if there's no brilliance in you, no flicker. Then you suck up the light.'

On the boat ride home, Marie held the cloth in her hand, buried in her pocket. Once home, she went to her room and put it in her sock and underwear drawer. She would, for the rest of her life, associate the smell of fresh laundry with a little bit of death; every shirt pulled over her head would make her hold her breath and think it was alarming to be alive another morning. Some of her shirts slipped on, then it was quick, the alarm. Other shirts had to be pulled hard and at angles. Her head would get stuck. Sometimes there was a struggle in which she panicked and pulled the shirt back off because she loved everything and did not want to die.

The opening of drawers, the smell and that light weight in hand, would from this day bring on a commanding loneliness. This loneliness would tell her that she must do something. But what, she had no idea. How lonely they all were, everyone she knew. Tristan somehow got his hands on this hummingbird, when what he must have wanted wasn't the thing, but something like its spirit. He must not have wanted these few feathers and guts. And Tomasin was the loneliest, dropping the body as if it were too much to hold, weighing a sugar cube or two, and it would weigh less as it dried out.

In the middle of the night, Marie awoke and opened the drawer a few inches.

The next morning, she took the loosely wrapped hummingbird out and placed it on her windowsill with her other prizes: the reminder notebook that was her diary (she kept only short notes, with no room for anything more), a copper cup with a hole shot in its side that she'd found in the water at a campsite, a piece of driftwood like a bird's wing, which she was always, every day, trying to find a match for, to make a pair, and a pitcher-plant shell from her father.

Keb had invited her to look for beaver houses in the marsh a bay away. He wanted to trap the beavers because they were coming in the night and chewing down all the saplings on their island. Sometimes they took a big tree. Marie walked beside her father across the bog, the ground soft and giving underfoot, and if she thought about it now, she could feel her shoes breaking through the grassy topsoil, sticking ankle-deep in the muck. The bog was a mat of wind-woven grasses and sticks, mosses and flowers afloat over a shallow, stagnant pool. The water was gelatinous, jelloed thick with plant refuse and leeches. This is where the moose came to feed. They'd found a dead moose half-submerged, its hulking shoulder rotting. It smelled so awful she had to put her shirt over her mouth, and when that didn't work she put her shirt in her mouth, which also didn't work. Everything was softening to a paste. Keb picked the pitcher plant and said, 'Marie, do you want this?' She said yes, saving it from becoming one with the moose shoulder.

'There's wind here, but the trees don't move. Do you see?' he said. 'The flowers don't move either.'

Marie wasn't sure.

'You can blow on them, and nothing.' He told her it was like this in some of the marshes.

'No,' she said, so he wouldn't think she was a sucker.

Then she blew on some tall grasses but they didn't bend. Until that day, she had no idea her father believed in things like that.

The pitcher plant was the same shape and size as the hummingbird, but hollow. It had the same weight. She could have poured out the change she kept in it and slipped the bird into the mouth of the shell, if it weren't for the stuck wing. She would have slipped it in whole, holding it by the tail.

After several days of putting the hummingbird in her drawer at night, then on the windowsill by day, Marie dug a hole in the ground. She dug it down by the dock in the early morning before her parents were awake. She had tried to love it like the pitcher plant, the driftwood, and the copper cup, but it bothered her. It seemed to weigh less and less, evaporating like a glass of water by the bedside. And who was drinking it up? Was the air nipping at it? If it was the air, did that mean she was breathing the hummingbird in?

On her knees beside the hole, Marie tried a last time to close the wing. It didn't seem right to bury a body that was bent. 'You don't want to stagger in there,' she said, about heaven, running her fingers along the tight small feathers of the bird's back. This bird was like an open pair of scissors. She squeezed until a bone or two broke like sugar sticks, more easily than she'd imagined. 'I'm not worried,' she said, thumbing the red throat. 'They give you new wings.'

The guides took turns fishing off the dock, and it was Tristan's turn for casting lessons at five o'clock. Five wasn't a good time. The bass were stuffed from hunting in full sun. If you managed to catch one, its fight would lag and it would rise to the surface throwing up wan, shredded, half-digested minnows, little pieces of flesh that looked like they'd been run through a washing machine. The walleye didn't rise to the surface to feed until dusk, two or three hours from now, and even then they couldn't be caught off the dock, only in less trespassed waters. The lake trout were at fifty feet, too deep for casting.

The interest for him wasn't in the fish, but in seeing if the people would be defeated by reaching out and touching nothing. Four women tightly dressed faced the water. The first three held their bodies with apprehension, as if anything might happen to them and they couldn't be ready. They were pretending to be more nervous than they were because that was fun. The fourth, standing at the far end of the dock, away from him, was much taller and stranger than the others. It was hard to tell if she was a woman or a girl. Her face was a young woman's, fresh under the eyes. Her dark brown hair tied back under her hat was, Tristan had to think, a lot like his. But her shoulders and back were all bonework. Under a loose white shirt, they called fossils to mind. It was Stella, but he didn't know that.

The first three held their fishing poles away from their bodies. They didn't make a move without instruction. But this one, at the end, looked down over the edge and held her pole close to her body, running the line through her fingers to feel if it was brittle or smooth. He always checked his line like that. He guessed she could cast as far as he could.

The sky was a tableau to the north, with clouds blooming like it was their last chance before a frost. As they bloomed, they grew darker, rose and twisted in conflicting winds, and would come to ground. These clouds would be as tenacious in crumbling as they were in building up like this.

He saw it coming. He knew she saw it too. There was no wind blowing across the dock, but there would be.

'Let's collect ourselves,' he said, ready to begin.

'If I collect myself, I'll die,' said Stella impatiently, but no one could hear. 'There's no question anymore,' she said, 'there never was. I used to collect things, but they fall apart.' It gave her pleasure to say so. That no one could hear made it better.

Tristan took his pole and shook it to show its give. 'When you're ready,' he told them, looking over the water, 'you can cast from this side or the other.' And as he spoke, he showed them, but with his lure fastened a couple feet out. 'You can be casual and flick your wrist.' He flicked his wrist. 'Or you can shift your weight and throw yourself into it.' He opened his stance and showed them what he meant.

People always wanted her to think and feel for them. Here, on this dock, she had only to feel the wind that was coming. Sometimes she didn't want even this much responsibility. The wind was indifferent, but it took her over. Most people would not have felt it or seen it in the trees, but Stella was sensitive to her solitude breached: the more subtle the breach, the more she perceived it. And this wind was false in its warmth. All winds carried messages. She knew the rain would be cold today. The wind's warmth was a sleight of hand; if she was taken in by it, she would only be more cold in the end. If she missed home, the deep south of her childhood – and she didn't, knowing nothing softens the brain like nostalgia – if she missed home, she missed the rain. In the morning if it rained, it was warm rain. In the afternoon, warm rain. In the middle of the night, at three or four, raining as she was coming home from the bar: warm as blood. Maybe not always, but that's how she remembered it. In the city now, even if the air was ninety degrees and the trees were labouring to breathe, and everything metal – from her earrings to the taxi door handle – burned to touch, the rain still fell cold. Cold rain didn't bring anything. It brought relief from the heat, physical relief, but no soul's respite. It didn't smell of plants and animals. It didn't bring the children outside.

Stella ran the line through her fingers and felt capable of doing something beautiful easily. 'Maybe the rain will wash me away and I'll miss my chance,' she said, still only to herself. 'Where will I wash up? Will there be others? I don't want to be followed.' She rocked a little at the edge of the dock, making the others nervous, which she could feel and liked. 'Maybe I won't get washed out, I'll be a shore.' Here was the question she'd been looking for, seeing the sky in the water. 'Maybe I won't feel anything then?' She felt a few drops of rain.

'You can watch,' Tristan said, his voice timorous but body sure as he swung his pole behind his back and whiplashed it forward. He let go of the line with a light snap and his lure flew low over the water.

She didn't look at him but knew he was there, a boy, and there were the others but they didn't have anything to do with her. She could see through them like shadows, even walk through them. She could step over them without lifting her knee high.

The other women tried. Stella and Tristan watched them, Stella with disgust and Tristan with some concern that they would soon blame him for not being able to do it.

Stella and Tristan saw each other through the others but made no sign there was something they shared. Independently but at the same time, it struck them through. They didn't know each other but didn't like each other, and maybe hated each other. Stella wanted him to be negligible and Tristan wanted her to go back to where she came from. He couldn't see her face clearly under her hat – he wanted to and didn't want to. Another afternoon and they might not have been so quick to feel defensive, such natural enemies, but the sky abloom was like music urging them to feel more right now – not to wait, but to do it, as the clouds broke into a downpour of raindrops, the first few huge, hitting the dock like wads of spit.

Stella stopped rocking. Tristan put his hands in his pockets, something he never did. Don't look at me, he thought. Why was she looking at him? Who do you think you are? she wanted to ask, feeling him recognize her. He recognized her whole way of being, a ruse to make people keep their distance. It was in him to do the same thing.

Stella lowered the drag on her reel and pulled out a generous lead. The first thing she felt was the weight of her lure and it pleased her, heavy enough to carry far.

The other women watched in admiration as she went through a motion so practised she might have been running her hands through her hair.

Behind the dock were shrubs with branches worn bare by the constant rinse of waves. They were more like piles of wire than living and breathing things. On her backswing, Stella's lure touched them, and to touch was to be caught.

She snagged. It was a common mistake, but the breath it held back was uncommon and she sighed.

The other women echoed her sigh, an obedient choir ready to do her bidding.

Tristan almost sighed with them, but covered his mouth and yawned instead.

Sighing wasn't something he did.

'Mother of god,' Stella said, pulling hard to free her lure.

She might have taken out some slack, but instead pulled so hard her pole bent like a ready bow.

The boy was saying something now, but of no use to her. 'I'll get it!' he was saying. He was here.

To make him get back, Stella pulled harder.

Drops of rain struck her face and hands. It was cold rain.

She pulled so hard her line might snap. She could feel it stretch. 'I'm getting it,' the boy told her. But she was getting it.

When her pole whiplashed, her body relaxed, understanding it was over – at the end of her line was nothing but a spit of air.

But the line hadn't broken. The lure was let go wild and precise as a slingshot. The hooks shook against the body of the lure, they all heard it. Then the hooks were silent, they heard that too. The lure didn't strike so much as stick under the eye, sinking into the ridge of her cheekbone. The hooks sunk in the way the prongs of a fork sink and disappear into a cake to see if it's cooked through the middle. But unlike the fork, which slips out when you pull up, the hooks were barbed, and if pulled now would tear her cheek apart.

Tristan came up close to her.

'I said cut the line,' she told him calmly.

She hadn't said to cut the line, but Tristan understood what she was telling him: he shared the blame.

He took out his pocket knife and worked on cutting the line. It wasn't quick work because he needed to be careful not to pull on the hooks curled into her skin.

'What are you doing?'

'I'm being careful,' he told her.

The rain was coming down now and his hands were wet and shaking too, because they were so close.

When the line fell away, she stepped back and told him to find someone.

He would, he said, but he didn't turn to go. He couldn't stop taking looks at the lure hanging off her face. It was one of his, a minnow crankbait, black-bodied with a gold stripe down the back, head to tail. It had fleck orange eyes.

Tomasin knocked on the door of Stella's cabin and told them, 'You can use me?' and they let her in.

Tristan was leaning against the wall behind the door. When she saw him, she pressed on the door to push it against him.

He had stayed so that no one could say he'd run away.

Emiel was standing in the middle of the room, loosely beside his father who was smoking and ashing on the cabin floor.

Keb was kneeling next to the bed. He was no doctor but knew how to get hooks out of hands. He'd never done a face.

'That lantern throws more heat than light,' he said. 'Go to the lodge and get the big flashlight.' He was talking to Tomasin.

But she didn't want to leave now that she was in. 'It's raining,' she said.

'You're wet from coming here.' He didn't look at her as he spoke. He was taking the body of the lure off the hooks. He clipped the two connecting rings one by one, with a pop from the pliers as each ring broke. When the hookless plug fell near Stella's mouth, Keb picked it up and put it in his pocket.

Tomasin wanted the lure for herself.

Keb wasn't a fisherman, Tristan knew. He wondered if he could pull the lure out of his pocket, and, yes, he thought he could.

Tomasin kept pressing against the door. She was helping Tristan to understand something, she always was. This was the woman who had taken her away from him, he realized, and his hatred of her at first sight made sense. He should have known down at the dock. She didn't belong, this woman. That's what Tomasin liked. He didn't belong either, but he didn't have a choice. Maybe he had had a choice once, but Tomasin had made it for him, and was still doing it, even now, though she wasn't trying anymore. She was implicating him. She was pressing against the door, pinning him. But she wouldn't look at him.

Tomasin wanted to stay because Stella was held down. She could be studied. Her hands resting on her ribs rose slowly with her breath, then quickly fell. She inhaled like she was saying something, but exhaled like she was spitting on the ground to get something out of her mouth. Her ribs weren't buried but peaked to form a ridge down from which her stomach sloped to her belt. Tomasin wondered if her own stomach did the same thing. She would have to lie down. Someone would have to look and tell her.

Stella didn't like seeing her doctor around and about, and she'd seen Keb almost every day. She liked her doctors anonymous. She also liked them in clean clothes, or at least clothes bought in the last decade. If they smelled, doctors were supposed to smell mildly of soap or antiseptic. If they smelled of sweat, they were too much like men. She felt his hands, the skin callused like canvas layered in paint. Skin so hard it cracked without irritation. Keb's hands were abstractions of hands. A doctor's hands were supposed to be gently shaped, lithe, and fit to hold delicate instruments. Keb was holding rubber-grip pliers.

'I can fix it,' he told her.

She didn't like that idea, to fix a face.

'We can't pull them out. They're too far gone, the barbs are sunk into the fat of your cheek, maybe the muscle. We'll push them through one by one, then we'll clip off the barbs and slip out the hook stumps.'

The cabin was small enough that she and Stella were sharing the air they breathed – Tomasin didn't acknowledge to herself that she was sharing the air with anyone else; she didn't admit the air tasted like a mixed drink of wet clothes and sweat – Keb's sweat, Tristan's sweat – and fetid smoke from Richter's cigarette and the potbelly stove burning wet.

'Go get the light. I'm not going to say it again,' Keb told her.

Tomasin pressed the door against Tristan one more time, as hard as she could, then jumped down the cabin steps and started running, reckless on the wet rocks of the path.

In the city, when her lovers woke, Stella was already out of bed. She needed to be on her feet, to stand a critical distance from everyone. There was math in how she held herself, in how she came over to you close, then turned. There was math in how she made you wonder if her effect on you was pointed, or your misreading. There was no math in lying down like this. There was no math here.

'Don't worry,' said Richter, looking at the hooks curl into her cheek, 'you still look good.' He gave her a sip of something out of his flask.

Stella could tell he was lying by the way he was sucking on his cigarette. She wanted to tell him to fuck himself. She wanted to tell Emiel to get rid of his father.

'This is going to be good for you. Your face will have a little more character,' Richter said, blowing his smoke across her.

Stella admitted something she'd been delaying to admit, because it was inconvenient. Richter was the most tedious lover she'd ever had. She would tell him. It wasn't the kind of thing to think and not tell.

When Tomasin came back with the flashlight, Keb told her to climb up on the bed and hold it. She pulled her shorts high to bend her knees freely and crawled until she was kneeling over Stella's head. It felt tight, like two people in a telephone booth. At home, she'd gone into the telephone booth downtown with friends. They told themselves they did it to find out who was claustrophobic, but they did it to press their bodies together. She could see tacky black stuff at the sides of Stella's eyes. It was mascara, but where it had clumped and dried it looked like tiny black flies. She put the light down and dabbed at the clumps with the bottom of her shirt.

'Richter, more,' said Keb, meaning give Stella more to drink.

Richter was the last person Stella wanted feeding her.

Keb took her chin and turned her head to touch Tomasin's knee. Her nose and lips lightly pressed against it. The knee was bare except for the finest blond hairs. The knee was also faintly sweet-smelling, Stella found, how chocolate smells through its wrapper.

Keb could have been brocading his name, so pleased yet so slowly he worked with his big hands.

Stella tried to feel only the girl's knee as the barbs were pushed through her cheek and clipped with loud pops of the tool.

Barbless, the hooks slipped back out like earrings, leaving two red holes each: the hole of entry and the hole Keb had punched to bring the barb to surface.

'That's the carnage,' Keb said, showing the others by pointing to the dots: six total. Her skin was swollen grey-pink around them.

'Is there a mirror?' asked Richter. 'Emiel, find a mirror.'

'There isn't a mirror,' said Emiel, who liked to look in a mirror and knew there were no mirrors in these cabins.

'I said find one,' Richter said.

'No,' said Stella, opening her eyes to tell him. 'Richter, leave me alone.'

'You can get down,' Keb told Tomasin.

But didn't he see Stella's hand on top of her knee? Tomasin wasn't going to move.

'Help her get into dry clothes and get clean sheets. Put them on the bed.'

She didn't want the hand to come off.

'Are you hearing me?'

'Am I a cabin girl now?' said Tomasin.

'Am I a doctor?' said Keb.

'Do you know Emiel? He'll help you,' said Richter, interrupting them. Stella had become Emiel's responsibility, not his. He wanted the flashlight and took it from the girl.

Keb didn't leave with Richter, but stood at the door until the beam of the flashlight disappeared.

With Keb gone, Tomasin suddenly remembered Tristan. She hadn't noticed him leave from his hiding place behind the door.

Stella lay in a ruined bed, the sheets and her clothes soaked from rain and sweat. She'd knocked her pillow on the floor. Emiel picked it up, but it was too wet to put back.

'I've never seen this,' said Emiel, putting his hand on the bed and crouching down. He pulled Stella up. 'I think you're drunk,' he said.

Stella, though half-conscious, seemed sure of him. He said, 'Up,' and she let him lift her.

Tomasin might have been used to the way jealousy overtook her, but she was not. She wanted to lift Stella up. He had a face with no colour. Maybe he was sickly – maybe she didn't have anything to worry about. He would lift her, tire, and let go.

'She needs to sit up so we can change her clothes.'

'You shouldn't do that,' said Tomasin. 'I'll do it.'

'I shouldn't do what?'

'You can't undress her.'

'Of course,' he answered, putting his hands on the bottom of Stella's shirt, ready to pull up.

'Are you making fun of me?' asked Tomasin.

'I don't know why I would.'

'It feels like you're making fun of me. Leave her shirt down.'

'I don't even know you.'

'You don't know me.'

'That's what I just said. I agree.'

'Good.'

'I could guess,' said Emiel.

'Guess what?'

'I could guess about you.'

'Don't do that.'

'While I'm doing this, would you get the bedsheets?'

Tomasin wanted to do the shirt. She wanted to lift it over Stella's head.

'How old are you?' she asked him. 'Just so I know.'

'I'm twenty-three years old.' Only teenagers asked people how old they were, he thought. He would not have to guess what she was like; she was so young she would reveal herself to him.

'I think you should let me do that.' He was taking off Stella's bracelets now.

'Tomasin is your name?'

'I want to do that part,' she said.

Stella loved listening to them talk. Maybe Emiel was doing this for her – she would ask him later.

'It's useless.'

'What's useless?' asked Tomasin.

'Your protest.'

'My what?'

'I've seen her undressed,' he said.

This was supposed to end the conversation, but Tomasin didn't understand.

'When?' she demanded.

Emiel surprised himself by laughing. Maybe he liked this girl. She was proud but didn't know anything, and he had always been charmed by that.

'When?' she persisted. 'And what are you laughing at?'

He was laughing at a lot. 'Many times,' he told her.

She didn't understand.

They pulled Stella's pants off one leg at a time.

Stella pretended to be unconscious.

Tomasin cupped her hands over Stella's knees to cover their appeal, then slid her hands to her shins.

Emiel watched and let it happen. 'You're a doubting Thomas,' he said.

'What does that mean?' She would pretend to understand almost anything but didn't like being called a man's name.

'It means you don't believe in anything unless you can get your hands on it. Thomas wanted to stick his fingers into the wound of Christ.'

She had no idea what he was talking about.

'It's a story I've always liked.'

'That's nice.' She kept her hands on Stella's shins.

'You're doing it, look!'

'Maybe.'

'You know what, you can touch her, I don't care. I don't think she cares either. You just can't touch everything all the time.'

He shook out Stella's nightgown.

'How come the clothes are so crisp here?' he asked.

'We dry them on the line.'

Tomasin undid the back of Stella's bra, slipped the straps over her shoulders, and lifted it away from her body.

Stella relaxed her arms and let the straps fall down and off her wrists.

Emiel was careful to pull the nightgown over Stella's head without touching her face. 'We need a bag of ice,' he said.

Tomasin was in and out of the kitchen for the ice before Marie could grab her by the waist.

'Oh, breathe!' Marie called at her back as she ran out and down the steps.

Tomasin didn't turn to answer. 'I'm breathing!' she cried out at the night.

Marie didn't understand anything and never would, thought Tomasin, landing on the ground and stretching her legs as she ran, showing them off to herself but also hoping that Marie was watching her getaway.

Tomasin is a beautiful runner, Marie thought. She is a beautiful walker. 'But breathe more,' she said. She was too far and would never hear.

Marie envied how Tomasin made things hard for herself. It was stupid but persuasive – the way the kitchen door sighed as she opened it wider than necessary every time. When she let go, it banged and was still banging as she took off into the dark turns of the path.

Stella told Emiel, 'You like her.'

'I do not.' It was hateful for Stella to say that. She knew he didn't like other women.

'You do.'

'I do not.' She wasn't even a woman but a girl.

'You do, I can tell.'

'You're drunk.'

'Yes.'

'I don't know, but if you're so sure, maybe I do like her.'

'I told you so.'

He put the ice against Stella's cheek, then lifted her hand to show her where to hold it. She was supposed to be asleep but held it.

'Shouldn't we stay?' asked Tomasin.

'She wants to be alone.'

'Did she say so?'

'She didn't say, but, Thomas, I just know.'

They left Stella's cabin, and it occurred to Tomasin that if she kept walking, they would split up. 'Where are you going?' she asked Emiel.

'Why?'

'I'm just wondering.'

'I'm going to get dry clothes.'

'Really?'

'You should too. You've forgotten you're soaked.'

'No.' She hated it when people told her to change her clothes if she hadn't thought of it herself.

'No?'

'I'm not supposed to wear wet clothes, but I don't mind them.'

'Who says you're not supposed to?' he asked. Her father and mother? She was probably younger than she looked.

'I like it.'

'In the city, where I'm from, wet clothes are gross.'

'They make me feel like I'm on an adventure, and I am.'

Emiel was not attracted to Tomasin but was moved to kiss her because she looked lost. Her confusion was general; something particular had to be done. So he kissed her on the side of the face. 'I really need dry clothes,' he said, standing back. 'If you want to come with me, you can.'

'I'll come with you.'

They walked to his cabin without touching hands. Tomasin walked ahead. He could see the shape of her body through her wet shirt and pants. She acted like she knew what she was doing, never turning to look back at him. People usually acted like they didn't know what was going on, but knew exactly what they were trying for, he thought. Walking along like this could be like breaking code. Only here there was no code.

Emiel grew up in his father's theatre, camping out in the dressing rooms and sleeping on couches. Some of the actors kept house there too, and he kept them company. He liked a woman or man alone, not needing to acknowledge him. He liked morning time, when there were only two or three actors or workers talking and smoking in the hallway, wanting nothing but to feel more awake. He also liked the night, when a group might stay to dance to the radio in a tight space. He was adored as a boy. They all came to him when they could, lifted, carried, passed him, and gave him things to hold. He did nothing, but the way a prince does nothing: he represented something. Something like youth before youth – the actors were young but Emiel was younger. He also represented something like innocence. But since he represented these things, he could never casually have them, and by fourteen he was neither young nor innocent at all, holding a kind of clandestine court where people came to hang out. Stella came there, that's how they'd met.

By the time Emiel was sixteen, he was promiscuous and it was admired. He seemed ambitious, but he wasn't; he had nothing else to do but take lovers. He didn't often go to school and never worked. He decorated his father's apartment, taping theatre posters up to cover the walls. The fridge door was like a cold skin, and he put nothing there because he didn't want to touch it. When his mother had left them, she had taken all the books. That's why the bookshelves stood empty. His father considered what she'd done theft, and such a violence against them that they would remember it forever. They would keep the shelves bare in monument. Their new books and knickknacks, accumulated over years now, were in piles on the floor, circled by dust and hair, their covers curled. They were less like piles of books and more like mounds of leaves raked and slowly rotting. No lovers visited their apartment. Sometimes Emiel slept on the floor beside his bed. When he was in his bed alone, he couldn't stop thinking his bed was empty.

He put his hand on Tomasin's lower back as she climbed the few steps to his cabin. When he took his hand away to light the lamp, she wanted him to put his hand back.

'Can I ask you a question?' she said.

'Sure.'

'Stella.'

'Is that a question?'

'Yeah.'

'She doesn't exist,' he said.

'I talk to her. She talks to me. I touched her. You saw me.'

'What did it feel like?'

'What do you mean?'

'I bet you can't remember what it felt like today. Your hands on her shins.'

'Yes, I can still feel it.'

'No, you can't.'

He thought she should leave him now and keep her ideas. But when he opened his mouth, he said, 'I don't want you to leave yet.'

'I won't leave.' She hadn't thought of leaving.

'Stay here,' he said.

He went back to the lamp and turned it off.

'Are you there?' she asked. 'You turned the light off.'

It was too dark for them to see each other, but by her words he found her mouth.

Tomasin didn't say wait. She didn't say anything because she was too busy following.

'Tell me what you don't like.'

She didn't know what she didn't like.

He knelt down to face her waist, lifting her shirt and pressing his fingers into her stomach. When her shirt fell back over his wrists, he kissed through it. She could feel his tongue moving against her stomach, across her shirt and skin.

She tried to kneel too but he held her standing. She tried again, now by bending her knees abruptly, collapsing them. If she couldn't kneel, or even crouch, she would fall.

She kept trying to fall. He lifted her as she fell.

'Stay there,' he said. 'Stand.' And he said it again, 'Stay,' pulling her shorts off without undoing the top button, and he kept pulling until they were at the floor. He had to put his hands on her feet, one at a time, to guide them to step out.

And as she stepped, he started to kiss her thighs, with his hands held behind, and he reached in to touch her, but barely, with the back of one hand. Then he was sucking on her right hip, the bone high and pointed, moving his tongue around and under its ridge. And he put spit on his hand and rubbed her hip, then over to her low stomach. When he put his mouth between her legs, it was so wet that he had to take small swallows.

Tomasin didn't know what to do with her hands. She tried holding his head, but it was moving around and in a way she couldn't shadow: here, her hands lagged; here, interfered. She tried his shoulders but they were too low. She put her hands on her hips, but it felt fixed like a pose, and this wasn't a time for poses. All poses were obliterated by what he was doing. Her body was losing its symmetry, its sides, and maybe she was finally falling, or maybe he was sitting her down on the edge of the bed, now the ground. She let her hands fall, grabbed at her own thighs and scratched them, and tried for his shoulders again, but they were too low down. She crossed her arms, they uncrossed themselves.

When she woke the dark was unwavering. She was wavering hard. She tried to take pride in what she'd done, but this feeling: like her own blood was scratching against the walls of her veins, long scratches trying to tell her something: I'm trying to tell you, her blood was saying. I'm telling you, it said. But it wouldn't say more than that. Or maybe it would, but messages she couldn't read.

Why did she think of Tristan? He was in the dark too, she was sure. There was a boy beside her sleeping. It was not Tristan. If she wanted to find Tristan, then she had to go into the dark and be a part of it. Could she leave out the window? The lake was full beyond the sill. She might slip through the window into the water and swim away from here.

She fell back asleep on the edge of the mattress, trying not to touch Emiel. She didn't want to make him touch her if he didn't want to anymore, and how could she know? She couldn't follow anymore, she was alone.

Stella was asleep as Emiel came in, sat down in the chair beside her, and lit a candle on the side table to see her face. Her cheek glistened with swelling around the punctures under her eye. It would have been bad if the hooks had hit her eye and sunk into its oil, he thought. The cheekbone had saved her. For once, he thought, her cheekbones had done something practical.

'Who are you?' Stella asked, waking from the smell of the match.

'Are you hungry?'

'It's you.'

'You didn't have any supper.'

'Hunger's for the weak, Emiel. What are you doing here?'

'I came to see you. I didn't mean to wake you up, that's not what I meant,' he said, leaning away from the candle. 'You might have kept sleeping.'

'You haven't come to tell me you love me, I hope. At this hour?'

'No, I didn't come for that.'

'I can't see you. Do you have that look?'

'What look?'

'The one you get when you're about to tell me you love me. Your face gets hard and a bit ghastly, I don't know, like frozen meat. I could bang it on a counter, and nothing. Do you know what I mean?'

'No, I don't have that look.'

'The look of death, Emiel.'

'The ice pack we gave you is in the bed. I think it melted. Do you want me to change the sheets again?'

'I can't be bothered. How's my face?'

'You don't look yourself.'

'I look bad.'

'No.'

'Let me enjoy it. I have always wanted to be unattractive.'

'You can't.'

'I've always wanted it.'

'What do you mean?'

'People don't look at you then. They know you're there, but they let you pass.'

'You can't have that, I guess. So sorry.'

'What do you want, Emiel? Why did you wake me up? What time is it?'

'I don't want anything.' He wanted his hand back. It was in hers.

'You don't know what you want.'

The floor of his cabin was swept. He'd left her asleep and had been gone less than an hour. His floor was supposed to be awash in clothes and books. His clothes were folded on the dresser; beside them, his books were stacked in a tight column. His books, in fact, formed a pedestal: headless, but it stared him down.

Emiel broke the pedestal into pieces and fanned his books across the floor, along the base of the dresser, both sides of the bed, and a few near the door. The bed was made with the sheets tucked in under the mattress. He untucked the sheets and pulled the cover back. Tomasin didn't seem like a girl who tucked sheets in. She didn't seem like a girl who made her bed. More like a girl who lost things in her own room and never found them.

He chose the long front dock because it was built high over the water and sounded out his footsteps in loud knocks. Maybe there was a script for this; maybe he'd memorized it so deeply he was following it unconsciously. The knocking was encouraging. Maybe he did know what he was doing. At the end of the dock was a pile of clothes. This seemed to make sense to him, though it didn't. It was five o'clock in the morning – still no sun, but there were patches of stars where no cloud blocked them out. He couldn't see the water under his feet. He held up a piece of the clothing, a shirt.

At first the shirt didn't tell Emiel anything. He couldn't tell if it was a boy's or girl's. But then he put his face to it and the smell was unmistakable: it was his smell. He gathered all the clothes in his arms, leaving only her boots. They were black leather ankle boots with the bottoms cracked like old paperbacks. He'd never managed to do that to a pair of shoes. Before his shoes disintegrated, he bought a new pair. He'd never slept with someone who wore shoes like this.

Cradling her clothes in his arms, he went to shore and took cover behind a bank of rock, kneeling down. When she didn't get out of the water for a long time – she loved this, he thought – Emiel sat down on the ground, holding her clothes for warmth now.

Tomasin moved through the water quickly but quietly, kicking under the waves. She didn't lounge, but pulled herself in full front strokes, far out beyond where people swam in the day. She cut across the boat channel until the water was hundreds of feet deep below. Holding her breath made her remember how good it was just to breathe and she felt better, diving down to feel the cold water around her shoulders and down her back to the backs of her legs.

When she finally came to shore and pulled herself onto the dock, she felt clean, resolved, and very cold. She didn't want her clothes but clean clothes or new clothes. She looked for them, bent down and ran her hands across the dock boards. But found only the rough planks. She found the gaps between the planks, stuck her fingers in there. Then she found her boots further from the edge than she'd left them.

She leapt back in under the water's cover.

'I can see you, Tristan,' she whispered, surfacing. He was the only person she could imagine out this late.

Emiel thought she could see him.

'Tristan, you son of a bitch,' she said. It could only be him. She wanted to shout but the sound would carry up the path and into the cabins. It would unfurl in the ears of the sleepers like ferns at first sun, or like flowers. His name would bloom if she called it out. 'Tristan,' she whispered, 'I can see you.' Maybe he was gone.

Did she think his name was Tristan? It was possible. There had been no formal introduction. He held her clothes tightly against his chest, as if they were trying to get away from him, as if by some witchcraft she could pull at them. He felt afraid of her, this night swimmer, and held the clothes close. She whispered with her mouth just above the water. It was a dangerous amalgam: she was unreasonable and at his mercy. She was a teenager without clothes. He was holding her clothes, which her mother must have bought for her. Emiel dropped them. But then dropping them didn't make him feel better, so he picked them back up.

'Tomasin,' he said with restraint, 'it's me.'

'What?' She couldn't hear.

'It's me. It's Emiel here.'

'Where?'

'Here.'

'Why are you hiding? I can't see you.'

'I'm not hiding.'

'You are,' she cried.

He came out and put her clothes down finally.

'I was trying to be funny,' he said.

'I thought I was talking to someone else.'

'Is your boyfriend going to come after me?'

'I don't have a boyfriend.'

'He'll come at me with his pocket knife,' Emiel said condescendingly. 'Who's Tristan?'

Tomasin's feet slid along the laddered logs of the dock's front crib. She slid closer to him. 'I don't have a boyfriend,' she said, 'but if I did, he would come for you.'

'Who's Tristan?'

'Leave me alone.' She didn't want to talk about Tristan.

'Is the water cold?'

'I don't know.'

'Is the water not cold? It must be.'

'It seemed cold at first, before, but I don't feel it anymore.'

'How long have you been in there? Will you come out?'

'You're standing on my clothes.'

Trying to see more of her, he'd come forward and stepped on them and stood there without feeling them bundled under his feet.

In return for the hummingbird, Marie slipped a necklace into the bottom of Tristan's tackle box. He found it tangled in line and loose hooks, a necklace of white string with two metal washers. The washers slid down the string and tapped as he picked it up.

No one was supposed to give him anything. But Tristan thought that if Tomasin was giving him a peace offering, then he would take it. He knew her. He knew that if he didn't put the necklace on, she would put it on for him. So he tied it around his neck and tucked the washers inside his shirt, where they tapped against his chest.

All the time, he was waiting for her. Down at the docks, under the verandah where they used to sit, down every path he walked. Working out on the water was the worst, because he couldn't keep a lookout. He had no thought or feeling for doing anything else. People talked to him, but he didn't answer. He wandered the island hoping to find her. If he walked down a path and broke all the spiderwebs, he knew she wasn't there. She had seen him that night at Stella's. She had pressed the door of the cabin into him for a long time. She had crawled up onto the bed, kneeled over that woman, her shorts riding high, and never looked back. He tapped the washers through his shirt and they clicked and stuck, cool against his skin, and he did it again. The blood was rushing to his head from looking down, making it hard to breathe through his broken nose. He breathed through his mouth, wanting to spit or cry. But he would not spit or cry. He was busy waiting.

He was falling asleep, leaning over his tackle box, his hands in his lures. If only Tomasin had come, then he would have been able to stop this and rest. When Tomasin was with him, there was no such thing as waiting.

'I found you,' said a familiar voice. He'd heard no footsteps on the dock, but Keb was standing over him. 'Hello?'

'Here I am,' Tristan answered, picking through his lures.

Keb put a bow saw on the dock beside the tackle box. He told Tristan the island had burned through its firewood during the last days of rain, and gave him an order for at least three birch trees cut into four-foot lengths – more if the boat would hold it. 'Take one of the fishing boats,' Keb said. 'The wood will be too fresh, but they won't know the difference.'

The boy didn't answer, but he always did his work, so Keb left him with his lures.

The lake was a mess. Whitecaps hung over black troughs. The black and white clashed. Tristan untied and threw the ropes into the boat, jumping in without starting the motor. The waves picked him up right away, pulling him off the dock and threatening to ram him onto the island, but he worked fast and got the motor humming, opening the throttle all at once and clenching his neck against the whiplash. Tristan usually looked back to see his wake split and the island grow smaller, but not today. All he could do was get away.

He drove to the nearest huge cove and looked for a beaver dam to save work. The beavers chopped down birch trees to eat their tenderest branches and leaves, often leaving the meat of the tree on land to rot, or in the water, where the branches made lush shelters for schools of minnows and fish. Tristan combed the shore looking for these offerings.

There was blood on the stump of the first one, where the beaver had cut its teeth. The blood wasn't dark yet, so the tree must have fallen earlier that morning or in the night. Cutting at the base, Tristan knew birch trees were his mother's favourite, but not to burn. She liked the sound of their ten thousand leaves in autumn shushing the sky. She liked their leaves in winter, she'd told him, when they were only an idea. Tristan moved up the length of the tree, cutting it in pieces as fast as he could, making the bow saw sing. At the water, he stopped, seeing the whole head of the tree submerged. The branches weren't stripped yet. They were unbroken and billowed out like lungs, as if they were still breathing. The water made the shuddering leaves look brighter green. There was shade in the cove, but the leaves held an eerie evening glow. It was the glow of flowers just after sunset, or the glow of flowers at night by flashlight. It was the glow of a fire when you blow on it. Everybody talked about the wind in the pines, but what about the water blowing through these branches? And the branches of ten thousand ghost trees like it? When Tristan heard the wind, he knew it was more complicated than people said. He knew what he was listening to. He wanted to tell Tomasin.

Stella's eyelids were glazed like a breakfast pastry. Tomasin wanted to touch them to see if she could wick the glaze off.

'I'll speak with my eyes shut, okay.'

'All right.'

'It's something new, something I like,' she said. 'You should try it.'

'Sometime.'

'Anyway, you look pitiful. Do you have to come to me like this?'

'I was working. I should have cleaned up but I wanted to come here more than I wanted to get clean.'

'Your sweat's so particular.'

'Pardon me?'

'I remember when my sweat was like yours. I had flat shoes and spoke with an accent.'

'Who?'

'I did.'

'What accent?'

'I had to rub it out of my tongue. It was like a pulled muscle, you know?' Stella opened her good eye, then both eyes, smiling at Tomasin. 'You know, you should prepare yourself to come to me. You should come as if you might be coming to a lover. Come that way, and I won't be distracted like this, by your sweat and crumpled shirt.'

'All right.'

'You remind me of so many things it makes me sick.'

'You're supposed to keep your eyes shut to rest them.'

'I died young, you know. But it's not tragic. There are no tragedies, only things that happen to some people. I went from stealing cream in plastic packets, pocketing them for snacks a dozen or two dozen at a time, to a life where everything was free. I could have cartons of cream, and I did.'

'Drinking cream is gross.'

'Not when you're hungry. Do you understand me?'

'I want to.'

'That's good enough.'

'What happened?'

'I just told you. I wanted to be so rich and powerful in cream packets that I would have to be assassinated. I would be a great man, I imagined.'

'You didn't die, you just changed.'

'It's a kind of death when you don't go home the same.'

'Well, I don't want to go home.'

'Don't say that. Life's exciting enough.'

'I would die like you.'

'Don't, please. It's impossible to control. We never die exactly.'

'How am I supposed to do it then?'

'Are you listening to me?'

'I'm trying.'

'I wasn't talking about you.'

Jer LaFleur kept saying, 'I can't feel my hands.'

'He can feel them,' said Adrian.

'He can feel them,' the others said.

Tristan covered his head. He could see Jer's legs, his blue jeans wet and ragged around the cuff. He thought about uncovering his head and grabbing the legs.

Jer put his foot under Tristan's hip and tried to flip him over. 'Are you okay?' he said.

'Yes,' Tristan answered, grabbing at the legs suddenly, but more in affection than anything.

Jer laughed loudly, the way he always laughed, and put a hand on Tristan's shoulder. 'It's over,' he said between his laughter. 'It's over, ducky,' he said, using one of his family's terms of endearment.

'No,' Tristan answered.

Jer wondered what to do with him. 'Mercy!' he cried out, with Tristan hugging his legs. 'I give up!' And everyone laughed.

'No,' said Tristan again. There was something better than mercy.

The swelling around Stella's eye was down, the puncture wounds tight and dry, but she was drunk and forgot she was healed.

'Tell me a story to distract me.'

'I don't know any,' Tomasin said defensively.

'That's not right, you don't know anything else.'

'I can't think of anything.'

She couldn't rouse herself, not even for Stella. Her nights were days now. She never slept, only watched a small block of the night sky out the window. People followed the sun east to west, but few followed the moon. Tomasin did both. It was something she could do now that she couldn't sleep. The moon sometimes moved across and down her window like a tear losing its shape.

'I don't care if I've heard it before,' said Stella. 'My face feels hideous, the mask of Mephistopheles! I don't like to touch it. It feels thick. And you can't think of anything to distract me?'

Stella put her hands behind her head, and her elbows and the soft sides of her arms framed her face gently. Tomasin thought she was very beautiful and looked at her favourite thing: how Stella's bottom lip bumped out and she tended to hold her mouth a little open. The swelling in her cheek had come down and returned her face to its fearful symmetry.

'Win your pardon,' she said. She could always tell how the girl was feeling.

Trying to be interesting, Tomasin kept finding herself talking about Tristan. She told Stella that he was trying to hurt himself. He kept fighting against all the boys. He was trying to change his face, she thought, by having people hit it: 'A face isn't something you break in. You just break it.'

'The boy on the dock?'

Tomasin wanted Stella to condemn Tristan, because then she would feel better about doing it.

'He's a guide,' she offered.

'Is he good?'

'Is he a good person?'

'No, a good guide?'

'He knows the water. He showed me.'

'Where's he from?'

'I don't know,' she said, 'maybe here.'

'How can you not know that if he's your friend? Haven't you asked him?'

'I never asked him anything.'

'What did you talk about?'

'I don't know, I can't remember.'

'What did you do?'

'I don't think we did anything.' She didn't want to say.

'Will you bring him to me?'

'I don't see him anymore.'

'Why not?'

'We were just pretending.'

'Pretending what?'

'We pretended to know each other. People do that. But he didn't know me.'

'You don't know him.'

'I know enough.'

'Help me to understand,' said Stella. 'First you pretended to know each other?'

'Yes.'

'And now you're pretending you don't know each other?'

'Wait,' said Tomasin.

But Stella didn't wait. 'What did you do to him?'

'I didn't do anything. He does it to himself. That's what makes me so uncomfortable.'

'That's why you're here,' said Stella, liking this. 'You're full of feeling.'

'I'm like you.'

'No,' Stella told her, 'I'm not like that anymore.'

Tomasin didn't understand. She was too tired to talk to Stella today.

'Don't feel sorry for yourself.'

'I don't,' said Tomasin.

'You must suffer now. It's suffering time.'

'Don't you think it's wrong?'

'What?'

'Tristan and what he does. He says he'll fight then doesn't put up his hands.'

'I could argue either way. I'm good at arguments. Want me to judge him?'

'I think so.'

'Are you sleeping with him?'

'No, I never would.'

'You never would. But are you?'

Tomasin turned from Stella and went to the window. She didn't look out but at the glass patinaed by smears where birds had flown into it. Did Stella mean Tristan or Emiel? Why was she still lying down when her face was better? It was a late August day, the sun was weak but pervasive. The light seemed to come not only through the window but the walls and in under the door. Tomasin felt that if she leaned, she might fall through the wall, as if it were a curtain. Maybe it was a way out.

'Hello?' said Stella.

Tomasin put her hand out and it hit the wall, jamming her wrist. It was a day that said: summer is over. She felt stressed at the passing of another season without her consent. She didn't agree to any of this: to the morning, the wall like a curtain, her throbbing hand.

'Are you sleeping with him?'

'Who?'

'Emiel,' Stella said.

'You asked about Tristan.'

'I did and then I didn't,' she said.

'I would throw up but I haven't eaten anything. I feel sick,' said Tomasin.

'Sit down beside me.'

'Don't make fun of me.'

'I wasn't.'

'I thought you were.'

'So Emiel?'

'The answer's no.'

'The answer is also yes. I understand both things can be true.'

Tomasin poured another drink for Stella because she didn't need another drink. She spilled a lot on the table.

'Well, good for you,' said Stella, watching her and wanting to touch her to see what she felt like.

'What?' Tomasin asked, leaning over and wiping the table with her sleeve.

'We do what we do.' She would forgive the girl for betraying her. 'We do it to those who get too close to our animal souls.'

'What did I do?'

'What didn't you do?'

'What's an animal soul? Are you crazy?'

'No, love. I should be offended by the question, but you can't offend me.'

'I don't understand.'

'Because you don't want to.'

He didn't feel like dancing. It was one reason Emiel didn't invite Tomasin to come. She would want to dance. But could she? She was unwieldy in bed. She would grow out of it, maybe, but for now her legs had a habit of tying themselves up in the bedsheet, by what series of motions it was impossible to imagine. One of her arms was always pinned under her torso. Her hair was in her kiss. There were pauses. He waited for her. She came over after work and sometimes they didn't eat and grew hungry, felt unhappy, and didn't know why. His habit was to leave her in his bed when he went out later at night.

Tomasin listened to him get up, pull on his clothes, and comb his hair in the dark. He had very short hair and she wondered why he bothered combing it. What upset her wasn't that he left, she thought, but that he combed his hair. And he closed the door so quietly, turning the handle like he was tuning an instrument. Sometimes, after he was gone, she knelt at the side of the bed to feel the floor against her knees. She put her head down and spread out her arms and hair across the top of the bedspread. The floor needed to be swept – she could feel the dirt pressing into her kneecaps.

Emiel and Stella were at the lodge drinking in the afternoon, alone in the world apart from the boats crossing the bay. The boats beat the waves in a baiting rhythm they both liked.

'What is this? When it touches my tongue, it singes.' Emiel was determined to match Stella glass for glass.

'It does,' she agreed.

'Does it have a taste? I can't taste it.'

The bottle had no label. It was swish. Noah Coke charged eight dollars for one, twelve for two. She would buy more that day.

'I don't know what it is, but I like it,' she said.

'It works.'

'You need it for strength, Emiel. You don't look strong these days.'

'I've never looked strong, I don't know what you mean.'

'Do you want to be weak? That suits you?'

'You call me weak for your entertainment. I'm not, I'm fine. I'm just not strong,' he said. 'If I felt weak, I'd tell you.'

'You look a bit weakly.'

'I don't look like anything.'

'You look like a boy who's lost his ball and doesn't know where to find it, or what to do now.'

'At least I'm not unkind.'

She could be unkind. It came naturally and was part of some of her earliest memories. But if she was unkind, it was not for her own benefit. She did it for the people.

Emiel thought how he hated her smile but loved her mouth.

'Let's talk about something else.'

'You better keep drinking,' she answered him, taking another drink herself. 'I can tell you're unhappy.'

Her face should have twisted as the swish hit her throat, but didn't.

'How's your wound?'

'Keb told me I'm not allowed to swim. He says the water will soften the wounds.'

'You've been swimming, I guess?'

'I try to hold my head out of the water, but it feels best when you dive under.'

They filled their glasses.

'I don't like going under,' said Emiel.

'When you're under and you can't take a new breath, that's what I like. You get to feel how long one breath lasts. It has an arc: everything's calm, then it's not. Like life.'

'I'm not drawn to the water. I see that people are.'

'I swim to feel better,' said Stella, 'but then I have to get out.'

Emiel felt strongly for her and wished they could always sit and talk like this.

'When I was young, I could stay in the water for hours. I could stay all day and never stop for lunch. I was so at peace with myself. Now I'm not.'

'No.'

They tapped glasses to that.

'You look older today, like an old man.'

'Oh well,' he said. 'Don't look at me then.'

'You know who's young?' Stella asked, answering before he could anticipate her. 'Your girlfriend.'

'I wouldn't call her that.'

'What would you call her?'

'I wouldn't call her.'

'I don't mean aloud. I don't care about that. But in your thoughts, to yourself, what do you say?'

'I don't say anything.'

'If that's true, then you're unkind after all. You're unkind, too.'

Emiel put his glass down and rubbed his eyes. He was getting a headache.

'You shouldn't rub your eyes like that.'

'I don't know if I'm awake today.'

'So when you're not with her, you don't think about her?'

'I don't, honestly.'

'That's interesting.'

'I don't think of her unless she's here.'

'Where?'

'Unless she's right here,' he said, looking around. 'She's not here. I'm not thinking of her now, see? The only thing is, sometimes I wish I could do something for her.'

'Why?'

'She wants something from me.'

'Like what?'

'It's not me she wants. It doesn't have anything to do with me, but there I am, so she preoccupies herself. Here I am, I mean.'

'Here you are,' said Stella.

'An old man.'

'There's something you could do for her.'

'What?'

'You could bring her dancing with us. You could take her by the waist, not gently, and dance tonight for a long time. You should. Your father wants you to dance.'

That was not something Emiel wanted. 'Why not gently?' he asked. 'I'm not saying I will, but if I do, why can't I do it gently, Stella? Why does everything have to be hard?'

'If you're too gentle, there's nothing worse, Emiel.'

'You think she wants to dance?'

'I say you take her dancing.'

'I thought about it. She doesn't have the shoes.'

'Don't be so specific,' said Stella, finishing her drink by spilling half across the back of her hand.

'I'll do whatever you want,' he said.

'Don't do it for my sake.'

'Fine, I'll do it just because.'

'It's not right to fuck her ad nauseam, then refuse to take her dancing. You've turned it all around.'

'I'm not refusing.'

'And we're leaving next week.'

'We are, but we're not sentimental, are we? Why are you thinking about this girl so much? Are you okay? I'll take her to the dance for the hell of it, I will, but not because we're leaving.'

'You must be a gentleman, but not too gentle.'

'I'll do it for you,' he said with his eyes fixed on her mouth, trying to guess what she was going to tell him next.

'Do it for yourself.'

'I knew you were going to say that.'

'The girl, she complains.'

'And you listen?'

'Even if I didn't listen, I would hear her.'

'She complains about me?'

'Not exactly.'

Emiel got out of his chair and crouched low in front of Stella. He wanted to kiss her, but the last time he'd tried that she had pushed him in the throat with the palm of her hand. Her hands were hard. So were her arms. They were like the arms of a mother of many children.

'I don't care about her,' he said.

'Let me finish, now that I've started. It's important.'

'What could be so important? This sucks.'

'I wasn't going to tell you. I thought you should find out, but you obviously don't want to know.'

'What are you talking about?'

'The girl complains. I've been trying to tell you all afternoon but you don't listen to me.'

'All I do is listen to you.'

'She complains about eating.'

'She pretends she's sick so she doesn't have to work,' he said. 'She told me that. She idles. I would blame her, but we do too.'

'She's like us.'

'Not exactly.' He didn't want to talk about her anymore.

'Maybe exactly.'

'She complains to feel close to you,' said Emiel.

'That makes no sense. It annoys me when she complains.' Stella put her hand in his hair and pulled a little.

'I think she's in love with you. Just like everyone. And I hate them all,' he said. 'I hate them for it.'

'Not everyone, just you. And you're drunk.'

'You're insane.'

'I'm insane?'

'Say something that isn't complicated,' he cried. 'I don't want one of your riddles. It isn't fair, Stella, I'm not good at them.'

'I've been wondering if she's pregnant. Do you really want me to say that?'

It was the first thing Tristan noticed. She was wearing someone else's shoes and they didn't fit.

When Tomasin saw Tristan's silhouette through the slats of the floorboards, she tried to laugh but her feet hurt too much.

He pulled the string-and-washer necklace out of his shirt to show her that he was wearing it.

She swallowed her laughter dryly like water crackers and it stuck to the sides of her mouth and the back of her tongue. She needed a sip of water and to slip out of these shoes.

Tristan stared up with his neck sharply bent and held the necklace. He pulled on the string like he might lift his body up by it, as if his body were an anchor he could raise to her. The string dug a fine line into the back of his neck, almost cutting into him, but he didn't feel it. Or he did, but didn't care.

It was like they had each other by the wrists and were spinning in tight circles. They both felt sick and wanted to let go but feared the letting go. He thought Tomasin had come back to sit beside him, but she was upstairs. When would she come down? And why was she walking like a heron, with stick legs?

She wondered what he had around his neck and why he was pulling on it.

Their eyes met through the floorboards, with nothing to say, waiting for the other to do something.

Tomasin looked down and breathed.

Tristan did nothing but look back at her, holding his breath and the necklace.

Then she stepped forward and with one of her boots blocked him out.

'I thought you wanted to dance,' Emiel said, coming up beside her.

'I don't feel like it.'

'But you're here. Don't you like it?'

'I feel tired. Do you feel tired?'

'We should dance.'

'Why?'

'People dance in summer. I thought you wanted to come here with me?'

She went to lean on the end of the piano, but as she did, the music rose up, growling at her and scaring her off.

'You need something to eat, a piece of fruit? I'll get it for you.'

'I don't need a piece of fruit.'

'I can hold you up, come on.'

Trying to dance, Emiel and Tomasin brought themselves to bear on each other. They worried they felt too little, then worried about feeling too much, only to end up feeling nothing but a conviction that something bad was happening between them, they didn't know what.

Tristan watched her do it to herself. How many times had she told him that she could dance? Now all she did was get carried around the dance floor by an old man.

'I don't know,' she whispered at Emiel's shoulder.

He could tell she was hungry by touching her. She was against him but slipping down. Her dress was cotton, its only thickness in the stitches of the hem. There was nothing to hold, and Emiel suddenly hated how young she was. He wondered what he was doing. He wondered if he should hold her very tightly or let her fall to the boards. He was paralyzed, he was dancing. They both were.

Tristan needed her to come down from there. He needed it for himself. He'd been waiting. He also needed it for her. She used to be at ease, and it was in her walk, and now it seemed she couldn't walk. She was being held up – her feet a breath above the floor – and it wasn't like she was floating along. She was being dragged.

'Don't be surprised,' Stella had told Emiel. 'That's just painful.'

'I am surprised,' he remembered saying.

'Don't be ridiculous.'

He deserved it. What he didn't deserve was Stella's involvement. It had to be her of all people to tell him what was going on in his life. When she'd told him, he felt nothing, only wondered how he should feel.

'Now you'll have a past,' she'd said. 'Welcome to the club.'

He'd never conceived of having a past. He didn't know what that meant.

Watching Tomasin go, he thought about following but instead stayed close to the piano, where no one could talk to him. Girls lose babies, he thought. He didn't wish this and never would, assuring himself, but he thought about it. Because they did. If your thoughts never appall you, then you must be dead, he went on thinking. He didn't know the man playing the piano but felt they were friends. Every note seemed to last a long time. Every note singled him out and told him he was probably right about most people, if not everyone: they were beggars to feeling; feeling was their god, they sat at her feet, pulled at her dress, tore off little ratty pieces of it, begging to be touched in turn. There was a reason the gods wore no shoes in the statues and the paintings. People had stolen them off their feet.

Tristan dragged his feet to let her know he was following. When she started to run, he stopped and watched her disappear in the turns of the path. Rows of stones lined the path to mark its edge, and he chose one with a flat top and sat down. He wondered if it was one of his stones – one he'd helped to carry and set. It was a grey rock, no lustre. It was one of his, he thought, because they all were. Looking down the row, they were like gravestones. If Tristan came from anywhere, if he had family, this was his lineage, this row as grey as a day of slow-coming rain. The sky on those days was a stone. The stone he was sitting on was a piece of that sky, and so were all the stones he'd picked up and thrown into the water. He knew some things others took for granted weren't true. He knew he didn't own anything, not a stone. No one owned a piece of land, not a cabin, not a lamp, not the oil in the lamp, not the oil on his skin.

'I don't care what you think of me,' she said.

'I didn't see you,' he said, looking up at her. She'd come back to him.

'How could you not see me? You followed me here.'

'But you ran away. I sat down.'

'You're a faster runner than I am. You could have caught me.'

'I thought you didn't want to be caught.'

'Here I am,' she said, impatiently.

'I thought you were gone.' He spoke like he was afraid to wake someone sleeping nearby. He was afraid to wake something in himself. He had to give up before she would come back – was that it?

'So what do you want?' she asked.

He didn't think he wanted anything.

'You're religious,' she told him. 'Do you know why I love saying that about you? Because it's true. It's not even a joke, it's not funny,' she said, beginning to cry.

It was impossible that she should understand him. The problem was sometimes it seemed she might. Sometimes she did. He wanted to cry too, but couldn't, so she was doing it for them. He wanted to know if there would be another time together. What was he supposed to do if he wasn't allowed to think about her and wait for her through winter? It was about surviving time, being together and not alone. Did she know the end of summer meant fall? That's what he wanted to ask her. Did she know how late they were in making up? That she was leaving? Is that why she was crying?

'I talk about you,' she said, confessing. 'I don't know what I'm saying, but I talk about you all the time.'

'Why?'

'I talk too much. I don't feel well,' she said.

She was asking for permission to go.

'Don't go away,' he said.

Tomasin dropped to her knees, pushing off the ground quickly. And now she needed to brush the dirt off her hands, but since that would admit what had just happened – she'd fallen down on the ground – she didn't brush them and the dirt stayed matted to her palms. She spread her fingers out not to feel it very much.

'I don't feel well either,' he told her.

She fell again, but this time he gave her his arms to pull up on, and she took them.

Tristan stood at the door of Keb's screen porch. It was a long porch with siding up to his waist and screen to the ceiling. It was a porch that might have had a table and many chairs, but there was only one chair.

'It's you again,' said Keb.

'I've never come here,' said Tristan, pressing against the screen. He shouldn't have pressed like that, the screen could stretch or rip, but he liked the cool porous feeling of it against his skin. He liked how it separated them but only slightly. If he needed to, he could get through.

Tristan saw Keb's hands on the arms of his chair, curled and clenched like he was holding oars. He'd worked so hard with them for so long they'd clawed up. Tristan knew the same thing would happen to his hands.

'How are things with you?' asked Keb.

'I'm not happy anymore.'

'You were happy before?'

'No,' said Tristan.

'You can't come here.'

Tristan sat down on the steps. This way they both sat facing the lake, which suited them. It meant less awkwardness in the pauses of their talk. It meant the loll of butterflies at the shore flowers, illusions of loons on the bay, and waves drawing out the sun a thousand ways.

No matter what I do, Tristan thought, there will be these waves.

If he tries to kill me, I might kill him by accident, Keb was thinking.

'How long will you sit there?'

'I know you take my pay. It's the way a father takes a son's pay. I never complained before,' Tristan began, 'but I need some things. I need a tent, a lantern, oil.'

'Are you running away?'

'It's my money.'

'They give you everything you need.'

'I know.'

'You're a boy.'

He probably was. He listened to Keb stand up, then he was doing something, sorting through his pockets. 'Come here,' he said, calling Tristan in.

Tristan climbed the stairs and opened the door. Inside, he was surprised to feel calm. The closer he came to Keb, the more calm he felt.

Keb kept looking out at the lake, even though Tristan was right there.

'I need your help,' he said. He held up his locked hands. 'Today my hands are bad.'

Tristan looked at his own hands to see if they were still good.

'I've got bills here,' Keb said, running his thumb across his shirt's breast pocket.

Tristan slipped two fingers into the pocket and pulled out a billfold. The money looked dug out of the earth. It had an oily film that made it hard to pick the bills apart. Tristan thought of people taking rings off the fingers of the dead, and taking everything out of their pockets. He told himself not to think like that, this belonged to him.

§

He didn't know how the fire started. All he knew was that he needed to rinse out his mouth because it tasted like gasoline. Gasoline haunts the mouth more than something rotten, more than drawn blood. You can't spit it out. It only spreads and melts, but won't melt away. Tristan wiped the corners of his mouth.

His hands, he could understand. But how was the gas in his mouth?

He stepped lightly not to slip, picking his steps from shore into the shallows, and as he stepped next, sheet lightning spread across the sky, lighting the lake shore to shore, and Prioleau felt small, like a bedroom, like he could touch its walls. Lightning flashed again like a Coleman lantern swinging over his head on a hook, flickering on and off in the wind. He wondered if there was method in the flicker. The trunks of the red pines at shore were lit so clearly and for so long, their bark read like shoal maps. The flashes seemed to correspond with his next steps as he scrambled down the rocks. Then they corresponded with his kick. Pulling through the water, his hands fanned open like new leaves, or lungs, like his hands could breathe. What leaf opens in the dark? Every now and then, mistaken, one must. But the lightning flashes soon dimmed, subsumed in the awful glow of the fire building up behind him. He swam into the deep he dreaded. But what was dread for? What purpose did it serve him? From here, he could watch the island burn. Aflame, it looked like a sun rising off the water. It was the island as it used to be, without anything but their cabin on the eastern shore. The whole thing was rising. Then it started to sink. He didn't understand at first, because he didn't hear it coming over the water: the rain. It was a rain so penetrating he almost drowned with his head above the waterline.

It wasn't exactly a new dream.

He was working the front dock. 'Tristan!' someone shouted, but he didn't care. He wanted to know if he would be able to find Tomasin later. He would leave work and find her. He would not let her go.

It was the end of the idea of summer. 'These races are too timid to interest me,' Stella told Emiel. They were on the swim dock low to the water, watching two boats criss-cross the bay. Richter was running races with his friends, but without guides no one was confident enough to drive full throttle. The water was black, then suddenly green or a crude brown-gold – only a sheer of water over a shoal, shallow enough to skin a swimmer's knees.

'How soon can we forget all this?' Emiel asked.

'Tomorrow.'

'How soon is that?'

'I don't know.'

Tristan caught one of the boats and pulled it close to the dock, then let go without taking a rope. He would stand in Tomasin's way and see what happened. If nothing happened, he would keep on standing. He was practising now.

'Did you do that on purpose?' It was Jer LaFleur.

Maybe he had done it on purpose, he didn't know.

Tristan watched Jer get an oar from the side of another boat and use it to pull in the absconder. Tristan knew all these people were not the same – they were not all one person – but that's how he felt about them: there were all these people. Then there was her.

'Tristan!'

Jer LaFleur is shouting my name, he thought. It was all awful. He hated it, names and boats. He didn't want to answer his name. Why was his name something anyone could say, no matter how unfamiliar, or how unfriendly to him?

Jer put something in his hand. It was a rope and it was wet from dragging in the water. It was tightening which meant the boat was drifting off the dock again.

'What's wrong with you?' said Jer.

Early in the morning, he had wet his hair and combed it with his fingers. He had looked into his mirror and rubbed his forehead to wake and smooth it. He was awake, he was sure, he was standing there, the wind in his clothes, but it felt like he was in the water, treading, waiting for something else.

He needed her to come find him and say, 'That's enough, Tristan, come back in.'

Tomasin sat on the steps with her arms around her knees.

'She says she'll come out here and beat you,' said Marie.

'She won't beat me.'

'I know.' Marie pulled on Tomasin's arms but couldn't undo them.

'I can't, Marie.'

Marie didn't let go. She held on to the arms. 'You can't just sit here.'

'It doesn't matter. Because I quit,' said Tomasin. 'You tell them, Marie. Tell them for me.'

'You can't quit now, it's the last day.'

Tomasin was always dishevelled, and often unhappy, but Marie knew this was different. Today her pink lips were not pink but white, making the line between skin and lip hard to distinguish. Her lips needed to be moisturized not to peel. Her voice whispered through them like a draft at a window, something Marie could feel more than hear. Usually Tomasin's lips were wet. And she never whispered, even when she thought she was whispering.

'We're having a party. We have to bring everything down to the front of the island. We have to make place settings. Please, Tomasin,' she said, trying again to lift her.

'Marie, don't touch me,' she said so quietly.

Marie bent down and wrapped her arms around Tomasin's middle and tried to hoist her.

'Don't you touch me,' Tomasin said unconvincingly, leaning into Marie's arms, wanting to be held.

'You feel slippery,' said Marie.

'I feel sick.'

'I'll get you something to drink.'

'I can't drink anything.'

'You should try.'

'You don't feel thin, Marie.' She leaned further into her arms.

'I've never been thin,' Marie agreed.

'You don't know anything, you know.'

'Probably I don't.'

'No, you don't,' said Tomasin.

'I don't mind the things you say to me.'

Anuta found them in each other's arms. Marie let go and put her hands behind her back and held them there.

Tomasin did nothing but miss Marie then.

Anuta told Tomasin to get up. But rising to her feet, she feared falling back to her knees, already so painfully bruised. She could not fall down on anyone else's knees.

They were making meat pies. She didn't want to throw up on the half-made pies. She tried closing her eyes to regain her sense of self, but waiting for her in the dark were so many possible selves and not one she liked. She moved without lifting her feet, pulling them across the floor not to lose touch. When she reached the door, she tripped over the strapping at the bottom of the frame and fell to one knee again.

Did they know she had taken to falling?

They didn't know. They were sorry she fell.

She stood up and coughed over the railing.

It seemed that something had to give out, until something did. Her nose started to bleed. It bled the way it did in grade school, when she sat at her desk. She'd try to hide her face in her hands. But she'd learned you can't hide blood in your hands. Now she didn't even try. She felt nothing at the touch of the wet red. 'Tristan should see this,' she said.

Marie pressed a cloth under her nose. 'Slowly, slowly, tilt back.'

And Marie kept pressing until the bleeding stopped. Tomasin never reached to take over the cloth.

Stella and Emiel moved to a small table set out on the court. There were three or four other tables, but no one there.

'If only I could be one of the useful people,' she said.

'You're useful.'

'I am not. I look around and everyone is always doing something. It makes me anxious. I don't do anything.'

'You do some things.'

'Like what?'

'You talk a lot.'

'I talk too much. I borrow money. Mostly I sit. Or I stand up and move around in patterns indiscernible to anyone but me, and maybe you. I wonder what it's like to be useful.'

She wasn't asking Emiel. He wasn't useful either.

'Beauty has its uses.'

'Like what?'

'It inspires people?'

'It inspires them to unrest,' she said. 'Do you see that man? What do you think of him?'

Noah Coke was high on a ladder, hanging paper lanterns in the trees leading from the court to the water.

'I don't know him.'

'We always talk about people we don't know.'

Noah dropped a cream-pink lantern and it fell slowly like a toy parachute. They watched him climb down, pick it up, and brush it off gently.

Noah turned the lantern in his hands and thought it would be a good colour for a summer dress that someone like Tomasin might wear.

'Why is it that I never invite him to sit down? I invite you. He could tell me what it's like to be useful.'

'We insult those we love. I think you love me too much, Stella.'

'He might be a better companion for me.'

'And who else?'

'What about that one?' she asked.

He was walking along the low path, carrying full tanks of gasoline, one in each hand, stepping lightly despite the weight. It was the boy Tomasin argued against. But he was impressive. His dark hair tied against his neck framed his face and made his forehead and sharp nose startle like the first words spoken late in a day.

'I don't know him,' said Emiel.

'Tomasin knows him. But they are pretending not to know each other these days.'

'He's just a boy, how old do you think? Fourteen? But the way he looks – ' Emiel said, unable to finish. The boy held his head so bluntly, a way Emiel never could. He did it with confidence or submission; some opposites were so close it was hard to tell them apart. What kind of girl was Tomasin to speak badly of someone who had what she wanted more than anything else? It wasn't confidence or submission. It was something better: self-possession.

'That kid, he's not a boy or man. We don't have a word for him.'

'Maybe we should,' Stella added.

'Why?'

'Because saying it would feel good.'

Marie flattened out the creases and wrinkles in the cloth draped over the long picnic table.

Tomasin didn't understand why a table needed to be perfectly set when it so shortly would be ruined. It was like making a bed. They were in the middle of nowhere. Did Marie not know where they were? A made bed, a set table, clean clothes – these things were absurd against this background of waves, which was also the foreground. The waves were everywhere. She had tried to go on despite them, but they were tireless. The waves needed no sleep and nothing to eat. The waves were winning. And they reminded her of him. Had he defeated her? If he had, it hadn't been fair from the beginning. Tristan had the waves on his side, she had nothing.

She sat down on the ground to recover from Marie's influence. Marie's work and care were making things worse. The bottoms of her feet cramped, and then from her feet up through her shins she went into a kind of touch-and-go paralysis. It pattered through her legs to her waist, then up through her stomach, chest, neck, throat, finally hitting her lips and tongue. She spat on the ground to take her mouth back, but didn't do well and half spat on herself.

She tried to say, 'Marie, I can't get up.'

'What is it?'

'I can't do it,' she said, crossing her arms against her chest and bowing her head to her knees. 'I can't move. I can't speak to you anymore. Leave me alone.'

'You can't speak to me? You are speaking,' said Marie, reaching out quickly to catch Tomasin though she was sitting down.

Washing her face and neck at the sink and mirror, Tomasin noticed a smattering of blood drops on the front of her shirt. She took her shirt off, soaped it, and scrubbed it against itself. The blood didn't come out but left pink halos, conspicuous for their subtlety. She put her shirt back on, a statement against desperation. She would wear it to show them she didn't care.

She walked to the front of the island in bare feet, carrying her painful new boots, swinging them in hand. She would dance a long time tonight, she planned. She would keep giving herself to Emiel to show it was not hard for her. It was not a problem. She tied the boots like ice skates, very tight, to make the pain less.

Most would have said Tristan made no expression as Tomasin walked by in her wet shirt and boots that were too small, but Marie saw how still he grew. He didn't make a face, not a gesture with his hands. He didn't do anything. It was awkward to begin, then unnatural, as he held his stare at the place Tomasin had passed by long after she was gone. Marie wasn't sure if he was breathing. He should breathe. She wasn't sure if she was breathing.

Tomasin sat down at Stella and Emiel's table.

'It's you,' said Emiel.

'It's also you,' she answered. 'And you,' looking at Stella.

'Is something wrong?' asked Emiel, raising his hands.

Stella excused herself by standing, taking one of Emiel's hanging hands and squeezing it. She kissed Tomasin on the cheek but lightly and without warmth.

Tomasin was exhausted but there was something else, some sort of depravity in her mood, which she could feel.

Her shirt was wet and splotched pink, and Emiel could see through it. Her face was shiny. He didn't know what to do, had no instinct. He would leave a letter that said he liked her so well.

'So?'

'We leave in the morning,' he said, revealing his impatience to go.

'I know. I'm also leaving.'

'Of course you are.'

'I'm not staying here.'

'I've had a good time. Haven't you?'

She couldn't tell him yes. She had had a bad time, she realized. She was too weak to pretend otherwise. She pushed the table into him. He had to block it with his hands. And when he took his hands away, she pushed it again.

'I understand,' he said. He understood that she was not going to do well today.

She stood up to get away from the table.

'We'll talk later,' she said, but to the table. She couldn't look at him.

'Okay,' he whispered.

'I can tell you're unhappy with me.' She wanted to sit down again.

'I'm unhappy,' he agreed, 'but I don't know why.'

Tomasin walked to the lower half of the swim dock and sat down alone. She wanted to get in the water because maybe it would make her feel better. She would feel more herself, less them. She didn't want to be like them, full of contradiction. She didn't even want to understand them anymore. The waves lapped against her shins and she felt the cold of the water, until it was all she felt, and it felt good. She wanted to be like this: full of one feeling.

Tristan had taught her how to read the waves, how to fall in with their rhythm, not insisting on her own. He did it by example, telling her by the way he watched for hours that they were not as she had always imagined – not all the same, not all one wave – but temperamental, unpredictable, without rule. She urged the ones coming at her now to rise more before curling under, to break in a thick wash around her legs. She had never cared about the wind, but it suddenly occurred to her that there was not enough of it. There had never been enough.

He didn't teach her everything. Maybe she didn't want to know it all or even very much. Some things were supposed to be mysterious. Before Tristan, she had looked at the far shore without noticing how the clouds over the land cast massive moving shadows, patches of black like islands adrift. Clouds had shadows. But not before Tristan told her. Now their shadows were all she could see over the land, how they moved like a search party covering and uncovering it. What were they looking for? If they were looking for her, they were on the wrong shore.

She slipped in to her waist, walked until she couldn't touch the bottom, then stretched out and swam. She didn't cry tears because Emiel was unkind, or because of Stella, or even because of Tristan. She cried because nothing had ever felt as it should between her and anyone. She dove under, held her breath as long as she could, surfaced and dove again. The water hid her tears from them.

Tristan watched someone swim off the island. It was a girl swimming in her clothes. It could only be her.

Marie watched in admiration. She could never master the front crawl. It was something about the breathing. She couldn't breathe sideways. Where Marie breathed, she went, and so she could never keep her body straight like this swimmer. She wondered if she would ever be able to swim with such ease and so beautifully. If her desire to achieve it could be held back by doubt, was it truly desire she felt, or something less? If she desired it, then she would have been able to do it. Desire overcomes inhibition, this swimmer, going into the deepest water, was telling her.

From his table, Emiel watched from the beginning. He thought she was trying to make a scene, to turn people's attention, particularly his. He was wrong about her then and would be wrong about her in his memory.

Stella had come to think of the girl as timid, a disappointment.

The cold water and her warm tears met on her cheek and cancelled each other out, so there were no tears and there was no water. She would know when to turn around, but not yet. She was gaining strength, not losing it. She would laugh with them all about swimming in her clothes. She would ask them to come in too. Tristan would want to punish her but he would fail and smile and show open affection, because he loved to watch her swim. She would forgive in general. No need to be specific. She would forgive them all, and this way could forgive herself.

But the strength she was gaining was not in her body. It was something else. No one was more surprised than she was. Here I am, she thought, looking at her hands – at the beautiful way skin illumines under water. Skin stays bright, even deep. It was the last thing she would do with her hands, just look. She looked for what seemed like a long time, her eyes full but not with water or tears. Her eyes were full of light. Here I am, she kept thinking, wanting to see her own face for some reason, even a quick reflection, but there were only these hands, which were hers. She felt the longer and more she looked, that she was falling in love with them, these beautiful hands, and would follow them anywhere.

When she went under, Tristan thought he understood. She was trying to prove something. He waited for her to surface in a different place, waiting a long time. She was good at holding her breath. But when she didn't surface after too long, he ran and dove off the dock in all his clothes and boots. A wave hit the back of his throat like a fist. He tried to swim forward but his boots weighed his legs down so that his hips bent sharply and he started to slip back. The dock was right there because he had not moved, only tread. Reaching up and holding a dock ring with one hand, he tore off his boots without untying the laces and stripped down to his bare arms and chest. She was always trying to get him to swim into the deep water. It was not something he could do. Why didn't she listen? He never told her why he couldn't do it, but she might have known. She knew, he thought. His clothes floated and the water churned white and grey around him as he tried again to swim, wrecking himself against the water and air, all the same to him, and as a wreckage he swam, pushing and punching ahead, when he might have pulled. But that wasn't him, that was her. Tomasin pulled through.

'You can't follow.' He heard her saying that. You never could.

Born in Guelph and based in New York, **Jesse Ruddock** first left Canada on a hockey scholarship to Harvard. Her writing and photography have appeared in the NewYorker.com, *n+1*, *BOMB*, *Music & Literature* and *Vice*. *Shot-Blue* is her first novel.